Her Twin Cowboys

Cameron Hart

Published by Cameron Hart, 2024.

This is a work of fiction. Similarities to real people, places, or events are entirely coincidental.

HER TWIN COWBOYS

First edition. February 23, 2024.

Copyright © 2024 Cameron Hart.

ISBN: 979-8224312689

Written by Cameron Hart.

Want a free book?

Sign up for my newsletter[1] and get your free copy of Chasing Stacy!

One look at the stunning waitress carrying the weight of the world on her shoulders, and I'm a goner. I wasn't looking for a sweet little thing with auburn hair and more baggage than I can fit on the back of my bike, but there's no going back now. She's mine. I'll prove to her I'm more than capable of handling her past and making her feel safe again.

---

1. https://dl.bookfunnel.com/7wbqvhsx8r

Connect with me!

Check out my website, cameronhart.net[2], for sneak previews on my latest projects.

Follow me on social media:

Facebook Page - facebook.com/cameronhartauthor
Instagram - instagram.com/cameron.hart.author
TikTok - tiktok.com/@author.cameron.hart
Goodreads - goodreads.com/16081533.Cameron_Hart
Bookbub - bookbub.com/authors/cameron-hart

---

2. https://cameronhart.net/

Chapter 1

Jacob

"God fucking dammit," I grumble as I pull over to the side of the highway. The road is empty except for me and the asshole who just rear-ended me. This is the absolute last thing I need today. I'm already running behind after having to go to the next town over to get the right feed since our local store was out.

Usually, I'm a pretty easy-going guy, but we've been short-staffed around the ranch as of late, what with all the babies and family bonding that's happening.

Jade, the owner of Rivera Ranch where I work, has an eighteen-month-old who is a handful, to say the least. I love the kid, but damn, she has a pair of lungs on her. Jade just found out she's pregnant again, which means Noah, her husband and the foreman of the ranch, is in over-protective dad/husband mode.

Teagan and her husband, Knox, recently had their baby as well, thus we're out a cook and another ranch hand. That just leaves Corey, Zane, myself, and my twin brother, Isaiah, to do the majority of the day-to-day stuff. I don't mind, however, shit like this will throw the whole day off schedule.

I'm muttering curses to myself as I step out of my truck and make my way over to the piece of shit Toyota truck that has to be older than my thirty years. I'm about to give the guy an earful when I see a flash of long auburn hair fly out of the vehicle, and then the driver promptly stumbles onto the gravel, landing on their hands and knees.

The anger drains from me completely, replaced by the need to get to this woman and make sure she's okay. It's more than common decency, it's an overwhelming wave of protectiveness like I've never felt.

Jesus, what's wrong with me?

I've only seen the woman's hair, and here I am wanting to wrap her up in a blanket and give her some hot cocoa. By the time I get to her, she's already picked herself up off the ground and is apologizing profusely.

I know I should acknowledge her in some way, ease her guilt by telling her I don't give a flying fuck about the car accident since it meant I got to meet her, but I can't stop staring at the goddess in front of me.

She has curves for days. Her thick thighs and wide hips make my hands twitch with the need to grip them and dig my fingers into her soft flesh. My eyes follow the slight dip in her waist and then land on her gorgeous breasts. More than a handful. And God, do I want my hands full of them. Not wanting to be a total creeper, I force my gaze to meet hers.

Fucking hell.

The short, curvy woman has an incredible body and an indescribably beautiful face. She's sinking her teeth into her bottom lip, clearly anxious for me to say something. I open my mouth, but no words come out. Instead, I continue taking all of her features in. Round cheeks, pink lips, cute button nose, and big expressive eyes, the color of whiskey. I didn't know eyes came in that color, but they go perfectly with her long silky reddish-brown hair.

I frown when I see a gash on her forehead. The little lady is still rambling on, coming up with new and creative ways to apologize, but I cut her off.

"Are you okay?" I ask, stepping closer to her.

"I... What?" She looks shocked at my question.

"Your head," I motion towards the cut on her forehead. "Shit, beautiful, your knees are all scraped up, too."

"Oh." I look up into her eyes again and see the confusion. "Um, yeah, I'm fine," the woman says with a dismissive hand. "Listen, about your truck—"

"The truck is fine," I say, not even looking at the damage. It doesn't matter. This woman is bleeding for Christ's sake.

"But there's a huge dent," she protests, pointing to the caved-in bumper.

I shrug. "It's not important," I tell her as I step closer to her. She looks at me skeptically but doesn't back away. "This," I murmur, reaching out to glide my thumb below the cut on her forehead, "This is important. Can I call an ambulance, beautiful?"

Her brow furrows at my words. She winces, the motion clearly aggravating her wound. "No, that's not necessary. If we can just exchange insurance information, I'll let you get on your way. I really am sorry, it's my first time driving this truck in months and I'm not super confident with stick shift, and to be honest, I should have adjusted the seat since I'm short, but I was running late for my interview, and..." She inhales a huge breath after getting most of her rant out. "And those are all excuses. The point is—"

"I told you already, my truck is fine. Yours on the other hand..." I look over at the old truck with the hood crunched in, the front bumper nearly falling off, and a small crack in the windshield. And that's only the visible damage. There are undoubtedly some internal problems as well. "Let me tow your vehicle to the ranch I work on. My brother, Isaiah, can look at it for you. He's always tinkering around with cars and machinery. He's good at all that stuff."

The woman backs away from me even more. I hate every inch between us. Seriously, I have no idea what this feeling is. I crave her. Fucking need her. It should scare me, but I'm more intrigued than anything else. What is it about her? I intend to find out.

"Is this some kind of joke? If so, I don't get it," she says, her defiant tone making my cock twitch.

Down, boy.

The woman crosses her arms over her chest, unknowingly pushing those luscious tits up. She's in jean shorts and a simple black, V-neck shirt, but fuck, she wears them well.

"No joke, beautiful. Let me get you cleaned up and tow your car back to the ranch.

"Stop calling me that," she mutters. "And as for your offer? Absolutely not. You can't fix my car after *I* ran into *you*. That's not how the world works. If you don't want to exchange insurance information, that's your prerogative, I guess. I'll just be on my way."

"Wait," I say as I close the distance between us and loop my fingers around her wrist, stopping her from turning away from me. She jerks her hand out of my grasp but stops moving. That one touch has every nerve ending in my entire body sparking to life. Her skin is soft and creamy. I want to see if the rest of her feels as silky smooth. I'll feel every inch of her, then lick every inch of her, then litter her delicate skin with little bites to show the world she's fucking *mine*.

Holy shit. I have to calm down. This woman is doing a number on me and she's not even trying.

"What? Why are you staring at me? What's your deal?"

I wish I knew, beautiful.

"Listen, I can't leave a bleeding woman on the side of the road. My momma raised me better than that. If you don't want help with your car, at least let me take you back to the ranch and clean you up. That cut looks like it hurts."

She glares at me, trying with everything in her to scare me off. I like her defiance, her fight. It's been a long damn time since a woman has been a challenge. The longer she stares me down, the more her resolve weakens. She's got to be hurting. I want to be the one to make her feel better.

The feisty little kitten looks me up and down, deciding whether she wants to trust me or scratch me. I want both. I want her to dig her claws into me and rip me to shreds while she offers her gorgeous fucking body up to me.

"I don't even know your name," she scoffs. My little goddess is trying to be tough, but I saw a flicker of hope in her whiskey eyes.

"I'm Jacob," I quickly say, holding out my hand for her to shake. She looks at my hand and then up into my eyes. "I work at Rivera Ranch, just up the road. Please let me get a bandage on your forehead and then we can talk about what to do with your car."

Finally, she takes my hand. Goddamn. Her hand is so soft and tiny. The complete opposite of my large, calloused hands. "I'm Nova."

"Nova," I repeat, not letting go of her. She pulls away from me and stomps towards my truck. I grin, loving how she didn't agree to my terms, she just marched ahead like the whole thing was her idea. My feisty little kitten. She'd be fun to tame. I'd tease her with my tongue, keeping her right on the edge of oblivion until she begged for my cock. I can almost hear her whimpers now...

"Are you coming, or what?" she shouts from the passenger's side of the truck.

I'll be coming soon, alright. Hopefully in your tight, wet pussy.

Jesus. I shake those thoughts from my head, chuckling at her attitude as I make my way towards my truck. Nova is an inch or two over five feet, which proves to be a disadvantage when climbing inside. I want to help her, but I have a feeling that wouldn't go over so well. Instead, I stand close by in case she needs me.

Once Nova is inside, I can't stop myself from reaching for her seatbelt so I can buckle her in. She slaps my hand away, making me laugh. Nova just glares at me and grabs the seatbelt out of my hand, buckling herself in. I grin and close her door before getting around to my side of the truck.

The five-minute drive to Rivera Ranch is silent, but I don't mind. It gives me more time to observe Nova while she looks out the passenger side window, dutifully ignoring me. She smells like cinnamon and coffee; warm and comforting.

When we pull in, I dart around to her side of the truck to help her down, but she beats me to it. Nova really is determined to do every damn thing on her own. I like her independent streak. She sure doesn't take shit from anyone, and she definitely does what she wants, when she wants to. Her submission would be so fucking sweet and satisfying.

Nova waits impatiently by the door of my cabin, tapping her foot and everything. So damn adorable. I walk right past her and open the door, stepping inside and holding it open for her to follow.

"You don't lock your door?" She asks incredulously.

I shrug. "I know everyone who lives and works on the ranch. No need to lock the door."

"That's awfully trusting of you. Or stupid. Probably both," she grumbles. I shake my head and chuckle at her pessimism.

"Take a seat on the couch, I'll grab the first aid kit," I say before dashing to the bathroom and coming right back. Some part of me expected her to have bolted in the thirty seconds I was gone. I can breathe again now that she's in my sight. It's unnerving how attached to her I've already become. I don't necessarily hate the feeling, it's just unfamiliar.

I kneel down in front of Nova and hear her gasp softly when our eyes meet. I can't help but smile as I place one hand on the back of her calf to straighten her leg out. After cleaning up her knees and putting a large band-aid on each one, I turn my attention to her forehead.

The cut isn't as bad as I thought, but I still hate that she got hurt. "Did you hit your head on the steering wheel?" I ask as I dab lightly around the wound, trying to be as gentle as I can.

Her cheeks turn a pretty pink, and Nova closes her eyes. "No..." she breathes out, then worries her bottom lip. She takes a deep breath and sighs. "I may have been messing with the CD player in the truck, trying to put a CD in...and then the case snapped and I stabbed myself in the head when I..."

"Ran smack into my bumper?" I supply for her, my tone playful so she knows I'm not mad.

Nova nods but winces when the motion inadvertently pushes my hand into her cut. "Yeah. I'm sorry about that, by the way. And all of this is unnecessary. I can take care of myself."

"What CD was it? And who listens to CDs anymore, anyway?" I ask, ignoring her millionth apology as well as her weak protests about me taking care of her. I can tell she doesn't really mean it. I think she likes being taken care of, she's just not used to it.

"I'll have you know, that CD player was a pretty big deal when my mom had it installed fifteen years ago. As for the CD in question…I'll be taking that secret to the grave with me." She raises a sassy eyebrow up, daring me to say something else about it. Nova is proud, but also playful. Fuck if that combination doesn't do all sorts of things to my dick as well as my heart. Nova is messing me all up, but in a delicious way I can't get enough of.

"A beautiful woman with intrigue and sass. It must be my lucky day," I say, relishing in the glare she gives me. I rub some antibiotic cream over her cut and place a band-aid over it. I get the sudden urge to kiss her forehead, but I restrain myself. She'd probably slap me. And that would probably make me cum in my pants.

Just then, the front door bangs open and Isaiah stomps into the cabin. "Where the fuck have you been?" he growls.

"Is that any way to greet our guest?" My tone is light, but I glare at Isaiah so he knows to chill the fuck out before he scares Nova off.

"Guest?" he grunts before his eyes fall on Nova. Isaiah's hands clench into fists at his side as he takes her in. I know that look. It's the same one I had when I first saw her. It literally is, since we're twins and all. The possessiveness and lust in his eyes might make someone in my position jealous, but not me.

Isaiah and I sometimes share women, and now that I know he's as interested as I am, a plan starts to form. She'll be ours, at least for one night. God knows Isaiah could use the release after his ex fucked him over a few years ago. Hell, I could use the release, too. It's been a long damn time since I've been with anyone.

My brother mutters something under his breath and turns away from her. Nova rolls her eyes, making me chuckle. She's unaffected by Isaiah's rudeness, which makes me like her all the more.

She'd be perfect for us. For the night. Maybe two nights.

I hear Isaiah rooting around in the cupboards in the kitchen, making me smile even more. I know as well as he does we don't have any food. We eat all our meals in the main house or go to Roy's Tavern, the bar-slash-diner-slash-coffee-shop in town. He just wants an excuse to hang around Nova, and he's being his weird-ass self about it.

"Okay, well, thanks for your...*help*." Nova chokes on the last word. I bite back a laugh.

"No problem, kitten," I say, getting up off the floor and holding my hand out to help her up.

"I'm not a kitten," she snaps, getting up without my help.

Keep fighting, kitten. It only makes me want you more.

"Can I get your number?" I ask, loving the blush that blooms across her face, down her neck, and disappears into her shirt. I bet her tits are red, too. I want to see them, suck on them, make her blush all the way down to her toes. But not yet.

"Wh-why, um, what? Why?" she stammers, backing away from me. How is she both adorably shy and defiantly sexy at the same time?

"To check in on you. I'll call you later tonight and make sure you don't have a concussion or anything." I think she's going to fight me on it, but to my surprise, she rattles off her number. I scramble for my phone, typing in the numbers as quickly as I can. I have a feeling she won't repeat herself.

"Thanks, beautiful," I wink.

"Oh my *gaaaawd*!" She draws out the last word dramatically, rolling her eyes for good measure. I swear I hear Isaiah snort, but that would mean he's laughing, and *that* hasn't happened ages. Not since before Trish cheated on him. That gives me an idea to help nudge this whole thing along.

"Listen, I'd love to take you back to your car, but I have to finish up my chores that were sorely neglected thanks to your need to switch CDs," I say with a wink. "Isaiah will take you, right, Iz?" I expect both of them to protest, but to my complete delight, Isaiah agrees. Nova doesn't say anything, which is basically the same thing as agreeing, at least in her book.

I grin as the two of them make their way outside. "I'll call you later, kitten!" I shout right as she closes the door. I hear her growl in frustration on the other side, and yeah, my cock is hard as a fucking rock. Shit, being inside of her is going to be life-altering.

Something deep in my heart tugs and tightens. I have a feeling it'll be life-altering in every single sense. I'll need her for more than two nights. I might need her forever.

Chapter 2

Isaiah

I know what Jacob is doing by making me give this gorgeous woman a ride. And goddamnit, it's working.

He wants me to get over my ex. Fucking *Trish*. I'm over her. Completely. I have been since I caught her sucking another man's dick in the back of her car in broad daylight, parked at the local gas station. Turns out she'd been sleeping around since the beginning of our relationship. Real classy, that one.

I have no idea what I saw in her. Ever. Yeah, Trish was hot, but she was manipulative. Condescending. Selfish. I didn't realize how bad things were between us until it all blew up. Getting rid of Trish was a weight off my shoulders, which begs the question, why the hell did I put up with her shit for so long? I've spent many evenings with a bottle of Jack trying to answer that, to no avail.

All that to say, it's not that I'm hung up on Trish. Not by a long shot. It's more that I don't trust anyone anymore, aside from Jacob. I don't trust women and I sure as hell don't trust myself when it comes to matters of the heart.

"So, what do you do? I mean, I know you work on a ranch, obviously," the woman next to me blurts out. "I just mean...I don't know what a ranch hand does. Do you round up cows with your horses and take them to slaughter or something? Is that how it even works?"

The corner of my lip twitches into a rusty smile. Is she talking about cattle drives? She's clearly getting her information from an old John Wayne movie. If I were the type of guy to use the word *adorable*, I'd use it to describe her.

But she's not just adorable. She's feisty as fuck. She didn't fall for Jacob's charm, which wins her points in my book. She also didn't seem fazed by my rude behavior, which earns her more points. Not that the points count towards anything, seeing as I'll likely never hear from her again after today.

I know Jacob wants to have some fun with her, and he's hoping I'll get on board as well. It's not his first attempt to throw a woman at me, but it is the first time I've been tempted to take him up on it. I mean, shit, she's perfect. Thick and curvy. I have to stop thinking about how soft she would feel against my solid chest. It's only making the situation in my pants worse.

I steal a glance at her but immediately regret it. Her cheeks are flushed pink and her golden-brown eyes look so genuine, so curious, so fucking innocent. I didn't know women like her existed anymore. I realize I never got her name, I just grunted at her and then clumsily made my way to the kitchen in a lame attempt to be close to her but not *too* close. I know Jacob saw right through it, which is exactly how he got me to agree to give the little lady a ride to her truck.

"You're right. Silence is probably best," she says after I got lost in my thoughts too much to even answer her. God, I'm an asshole. I'm not used to small talk.

"What's your name?" I grunt.

"You're giving a stranger a ride? Isn't that breaking the first rule of *how not to get murdered by a psycho?*"

I feel an unfamiliar rumble echoing through my chest and then bubbling out of my mouth. She made me laugh. She actually made me laugh. I'll be damned. The thought of the beautiful, short, curvy woman harming a six foot three, broad-shouldered, muscled brute such as myself is undeniably funny. Despite all her bravado, I have a feeling she wouldn't hurt a fly. I can't help but steal another glance at her. Her eyes are brilliant, sparkling with laughter and a little mischief.

"Are you saying you're a psycho?" I reply, tearing my eyes away from her and focusing on the road again.

"I guess you'll find out."

I find myself fighting another smile. I don't even know why I'm fighting it, except that it feels vulnerable to show her this part of me I've all but forgotten.

"Are you not going to tell me your name?"

"Nah. Where's the fun in that?"

I'm not looking at her, but I can hear her playfulness. It does something to me. My mystery woman is strong and sassy, yet innocent and sweet. It's an intoxicating contradiction that I want more of.

Shit.

Jacob wants us to fuck her, not fall for her. But I can already tell she's not someone you have for just one night. No, this is the kind of girl you keep forever.

"There's my truck," she says, pointing to a rusted-out piece of shit Toyota. I slow down as we approach, trying to understand this nagging feeling in my gut. I don't just disapprove of the old car, it angers me. I don't want her driving it. I don't want her near it. I don't want her to leave me, which is terrifying and confusing as fuck. But more than any of that, I don't want her to get hurt.

"Need me to look under the hood? See if there's any internal damage?" I say, not wanting her to drive away in that thing.

She laughs, the soft sound curling around me, making me softer just for hearing it. I don't know what this woman is doing to me, or why her sounds, her words, her wit, and her curves are having such a visceral effect on me.

"You and Jacob are opposites in a lot of ways, but you both sure have a savior complex," she rolls her eyes but smiles brightly. "I'll tell you the same thing I told him - the accident was *my* fault, which means it's *my* responsibility to fix it. In no world does it make sense for you guys to clean up my mess."

Well, damn. What happened to this golden-eyed temptress to make her so defensive? I admire her independent nature and wanting to own up to her mistakes. Two things that could never have been said of Trish.

I throw my own truck in park right as she reaches for the door handle. "Stay!" I bark out. She visibly flinches and I growl at myself in anger. Of course, she flinches at that as well. I feel like a fucking animal and I don't understand anything that's happening to me right now.

As soon as I get out of the truck, I see the curvy little lady fly out of her seat. Damn stubborn woman. She's too short, she's going to…

"Ah!"she shrieks as she trips out of the truck.

I race over and haul her up into my arms a split second before she would have made contact with the gravel. My heart is pounding painfully in my chest, though I'm not sure if it's because of fear that she could have hurt herself or because of the way her body melts into mine as I continue to hold her tightly.

Her soft, generous curves press into the hard slats of my muscles, making me bite back a groan. God, it's been so long since I've held a woman in my arms, and never anyone as stunning as her. She gasps quietly and steadies herself by gripping my biceps. Fuck, her soft skin, warm, rich, earthy smell, and silky auburn hair surround me and make me lock my arms around her so she doesn't escape.

I tilt my head down as she tilts her head up. I'm met with golden eyes full of the same questions I have. Namely, what the hell is happening and why is it so hard to walk away? Her breaths are shallow, her eyes dilated, her pulse pounding on the side of her neck. I want to lick it. Suck it. Bite it. I want to leave my fucking mark on her. *Mine.*

What the fuck?

"I told you to stay put," I growl, needing to put some distance between us. The woman tenses in my arms and pushes her way out of them. Why does my chest tighten with each step she takes away from me? That's what I wanted, but I didn't expect it to physically hurt me. I can't leave her like this. The last thing I say to her can't be the assholish remark I grunted at her. "Wait, I'm—"

"Okay, well, thanks for the ride. Tell Jacob thanks for patching me up," she calls out over her shoulder.

"Hold on, miss…" Shit, I still didn't get her name. How the hell did this beautiful woman turn my world upside down in less than an hour?

She gets in her car and starts it up. The once quiet highway is filled with the loud cough and sputter of the old engine. A half-second later, I hear the thumping bass of rap music as she turns up the volume. It almost has me smiling again, despite the hollow ache in my chest. It's another unexpected layer to the golden-eyed goddess. She waves at me from her window, taking the sun and all of its warmth with her as she drives away.

"Shit," I yell to the empty road. I kick the side of the truck and swear again. It doesn't matter if Jacob has her number. There's no way she'd ever want to see me again.

The thought of her and Jacob together, without me, has heat and anger bubbling up to the surface. Yeah, Jacob and I have shared women before, and hell yeah, it's hot as fuck to give someone ultimate pleasure and watch them get completely obliterated by two big cocks. But it's only ever been one-night stands. We've never been serious about a girl. In fact, Jacob has never been serious about anyone.

After a few deep breaths, I've finally calmed down enough to get back into the truck. Another wave of jealously washes over me when I think about the two of them dating, getting married, starting a family. I always knew Jacob would settle down someday, hell, I nearly settled down myself before my whole life blew up. But the idea of him and the stunning, mysterious woman having a life without me hurts more than it should.

Am I upset because it's her? Am I upset because Jacob and I would no longer have the same bond we do now? The fucked-up thing about it is that I'm not sure. Probably both.

I grip the steering wheel so hard I'm afraid it might snap off, but then I relax my hold. I know better than to let my emotions rule me.

Jacob is the one who flies by the seat of his pants. He's the fun one, the twin who wears his heart on his sleeve. We might look alike, but that's where the similarities end.

One of us had to be serious growing up. Jacob probably would have flunked out of high school had I not been there to study with him and keep him focused. It's not that he's dumb, not by a long shot. He just didn't value the education found in textbooks. He's always been more of a hands-on kind of guy.

What he lacked in discipline, he more than made up for in social skills. Ever the outgoing extrovert, Jacob forced me to go to parties with him so I would stop being a broody, stoic bastard. His words, not mine.

The joke is on him though, because I met Trish at one such party. She made me the broodiest version of myself after she betrayed me. Jacob hasn't made me socialize since.

Ah, Trish. That's one way to get some perspective. I have no business being caught up in another woman, let alone a woman who already gave her number to my brother. I won't be played for a fool again, and certainly not against my own twin.

I'm mostly under control by the time I pull back onto the highway. I have a good life. I'm doing just fine without a woman, and I'll continue to do just fine.

Chapter 3

Nova

As soon as Isaiah's truck is out of sight, I pull into a little gravel side-road and park, turning off the music so I can think. My hands are sweaty and my heart is pounding out of my chest. I feel like I'm going to hyperventilate. I loosen my death grip on the steering wheel and rest my forehead on it instead. I'm shaking. Why am I shaking? Why can't I breathe? Who the hell are Jacob and Isaiah, and why are they making my entire body heat up and sizzle?

Yeah, *both* of them. God, who am I right now?

Like it wasn't enough to get into a fender bender with the hottest cowboy to ever walk the planet, but it turns out he has a freaking *twin*! I mean come on, that's not even fair. I barely survived getting in the car with Jacob and letting him clean up my wounds and attempt to charm me with his dimpled grin and straight white teeth. And then his equally attractive twin brother stomped in, all grumpy and adorable, and I felt like I had died and gone to cowgirl heaven.

Aside from their matching dirty blonde hair, green eyes, and ridiculously ripped bodies, the two of them could not be more opposite. Except, apparently, when it comes to my safety. It's kind of cute, really. I've been taking care of myself and my mom for pretty much my whole life.

Thinking of my mom waiting for me at home has me turning the truck around and getting back on the road. The old vehicle is a little worse for wear after the accident, but I don't have money to pay for repairs, so I'll have to make do for now. That's been a theme lately. Making do.

I hit the play button on the old CD player and let Tupac drown out my self-pitying thoughts. I blame my love of old school hip-hop on my mom. We might be opposites in almost every way, but for some reason, her taste in music rubbed off on me.

A few minutes later, I'm pulling up into the driveway of the small cottage my mom and I live in on the edge of town. I take a few more seconds to collect myself after my eventful afternoon and then head inside.

"There's my beautiful honey buns!" my mom's melodic voice rings out. "Come into the kitchen and tell me about the interview!"

"What are you doing up?" I ask, rushing over to the kitchen to see my mother putting a tray of cookies into the oven and setting the timer. She spins on her heel when she sees me and gives me a big, sparkling smile like only my momma can.

"I'm fine, stop worrying so much. You're far too young to have the weight of the world on your shoulders," she says breezily as if I haven't always carried the weight of the world on my shoulders. Well, our world, anyway.

"The doctor said—"

"Pfft," she waves a dismissive hand in the air and scowls. "Medicine isn't just science, honeykins. It's in the air we breathe, the energy we put out, and the love we give."

I'm about to tell her that her *energy* doesn't seem to be helping her battle cancer but decide against it. We don't need to have *that* conversation again. I'm just glad she finally agreed to surgery.

"I know, mom, but you still need to rest. You just got out of surgery ten days ago."

"Which means I've had ten whole days of rest. What I need now are cookies. Good thing we'll have some in about twelve minutes." She winks and smiles at me. "Now tell me about the interview!"

The interview. I almost forgot. "You're looking at the newest waitress at Roy's Tavern!" I say with all the excitement I can muster. I must miss the mark a bit because my mom deflates and gives me a teary smile.

"I know this is not what you thought your life would be like, honey bear," she says softly.

"No, Mom, it's not that. I want to be here for you, you know that. I never would have left if I knew you had ca—"

"Shh, now. None of that. It's okay to admit you didn't want to drop out of college and come back to your dinky hometown to take care of your sick mother. I promise this is not new or upsetting information to me," she says with that knowing look only mothers can pull off. "I wanted you to spread your wings. You were always such a serious little girl, always needed to be in control of everything. I wanted you to go out there in the big bad world and find your place. Your people."

"You are my people, mom. You are literally my only family," I laugh.

"And don't you forget it!" She laughs with me. "But you know what I mean. You had such a hard time in high school with that bully and I just—"

"Shh, now. None of that," I tease, giving her words right back to her. "I love you, mom. I want to be here. Now, how about you pick out which episode of Gilmore Girls we're going to watch, and I'll get the cookies?"

"More beautiful words have never been spoken," she sighs dreamily, fluttering her eyelashes.

I laugh and shoo her off, giving me some much-needed space. By the time I make it back to the living room with the plate of cookies and a big glass of milk for us to share, Mom is sound asleep on the couch. I shake my head thinking how I was right - she *does* need rest. But I'm just happy she's getting it now.

I cover her up in a blanket and turn the volume down on the tv before sitting on the other end of the couch. I remember the first time we watched Gilmore Girls together. My mom said we were like Lorelai and Rory - an epic mother/daughter duo for the ages. For the most part, we still are.

My mom had me when she was twenty-two. She always told me that I was the best surprise, and she knew we were going to be best friends from the moment she took the pregnancy test. It truly baffled her when I wanted to know who my father was as if it never occurred to her to even investigate.

Mom is a free spirit. We've always had fun together, and there has never been a shortage of love. She makes jewelry and does pretty well for herself. I set her up with an Etsy account a few years ago, which was a total game-changer.

While I love her beautiful soul and the carefree way she approaches life, one of us needed to keep a schedule. I was the one to make dinners and remind her to eat when she would get caught up in a jewelry project. I was the one who made doctor appointments and filled out the paperwork for school field trips. When I was in seventh grade, I took over the budget - or lack thereof, after our water was shut off for the third time in a year. It's not that we didn't have money, it's just that mom didn't care about the details. Putting the bills on autopay was one of my greatest contributions to the family.

I don't begrudge my mother for her ways. She balances me out and reminds me to take a breath and enjoy the world around me. However, I didn't have the most stable childhood. The day-to-day details were up to me, and I've carried the weight of that responsibility and need for control into adulthood, for better or worse.

I got several scholarships to the University of Oklahoma, but only stayed there for one and a half semesters. When I came home for a quick weekend visit last month, I found out my mom had breast cancer. She was diagnosed right before I came home for Christmas break, but she kept it a secret. I never would have left had I known.

As soon as I found out, I dropped out and officially moved back home. Luckily the cancer is slow-growing, and they caught it early. She had a double mastectomy a few days ago, and she'll have several radiation treatments. It was a battle to get her to even agree to a treatment plan in the first place. Mom has always subscribed to a rather loose definition of "medical care," which includes healing crystals, incense, dancing in the rain, praying to the universe, and lots of chocolate chip cookies, of course.

I knew she wouldn't have gone to her scheduled appointments if I wasn't the one to drive her there myself, so there was no other choice but to move back. I'm not bitter, really, I'm not. I love my mom and I'm happy to take care of her. It's familiar, at least. Plus, the big bad world isn't all it's cracked up to be.

Yes, being back here is not what my life plan was—the life plan I've had since I was in fourth grade, thank you very much—but I'm...making do.

Several hours later, I'm drying the last of the dishes from dinner. The dishwasher has been on the fritz since before I was home for Christmas break. I left the product number for the part that needs to be ordered, along with the number to call for someone to come out and fix it, but Mom never got around to it. I'll just add it to the growing list of things that need my attention when I find the time in between doctor appointments and shifts at the tavern.

I know it sounds like I'm treating my mom like a child, but in my defense, she acts like one when she's sick. Complete with a pouty face and a defiant stomp of her foot when I tell her to take her medicine.

I've never doubted that my mom loves me, but sometimes I wish she cared for me in the way I care for her. For once, it'd be nice to not worry about every little thing or to have the details taken care of before I even ask. What would it have been like to have a mother who brought me soup when I was sick instead of the other way around? Or held me when I cried? Don't get me wrong, my mom has always shown me affection in her own way. She's just not a big hugger or a fan of being touched, so she assumed I was the same way.

I don't think I am, though. Sometimes I just want to be comforted. To be held. Like Isaiah held me today when I fell. I want to feel seen, like when Jacob noticed my wounds and insisted on bandaging me up.

I want these things, but I don't know how to accept them. How to trust them.

Sure, the guys took care of me today, but how long can I really depend on them to be there for me? At the end of the day, I'm the only one I can count on. The idea of letting go, of being at the mercy of someone else, is totally terrifying. No, as much as I long for the level of care I was shown today, there's no way something like that could be sustainable in the long run.

I guess it's a good thing I gave Jacob a fake phone number. The sooner I forget about the twins, the better. I wouldn't know how to handle one man, let alone two. I'm better off alone.

Chapter 4

Jacob

I step into the shower and turn it on as hot as it will go. The water beats down on my chest, burning away the stress and tension from my muscles. It's been a long fucking week at Rivera Ranch. It seems like everything that could go wrong, did.

Knox and Teagan's new baby, Max, has been sick, which is stressing everyone out. We were overbooked for the event space over the weekend, which means we had to work double time to get things cleared away between the two parties. And then a fence broke on the north end of the property and we had to go chase down twenty head of cattle a yesterday.

And to top it all off, Nova gave me a fake number.

I can't help but grin as I turn around in the shower, letting the water slide down the aching muscles in my back. It's been a long damn time since a woman was a challenge. Right on cue, my cock starts to harden as I think about the drop-dead gorgeous woman who literally crashed into my life and flipped it upside down without even trying.

I don't fight it, I just grip myself and pump up and down my shaft, remembering her pouty pink lips and the fire in her beautiful, golden eyes. Squeezing my dick harder, I groan and imagine what it would be like to kiss those lips, to steal the breath right out of her lungs, and then spin her around and plow into her from behind while she begs for more.

"Fuck," I grunt, picking up speed. I picture Nova kneeling in front of me in the shower, opening her mouth and letting me feed her my cock. She hollows out her cheeks, taking all of my thickness down her throat until she chokes on me.

Precum dribbles down my shaft as I stroke myself harder, placing a hand on the shower wall to keep my balance. I imagine Nova teasing me, bringing me right to the edge, and then backing off. I grip her hair and shove my cock into her waiting mouth, pumping in and out, in and out, so close, almost there...

And then I yank her off and pull her up into my arms, kissing her until her legs give out. In my fantasy, Isaiah is right there to catch her, his hands roaming over her hills and valleys, cupping her breasts and massaging them. Nova whimpers into my mouth as I lift her leg up to hook around my hip.

I enter her slowly as Isaiah holds her up and opens her even more for me. Fuck, my dick twitches in my hand, throbbing, aching for the relief I know I'll only get from being inside of her soaking wet pussy. I imagine working her up, thrusting into her over and over while sucking on her luscious tits. Isaiah turns her head so he can kiss her. She cries out when Isaiah circles her clit and I bite down on her nipple.

"Jesus, Nova," I groan, my body tight, my dick swollen, my heart pounding away in my chest. Nova explodes in my arms, taking me with her.

Cum shoots out of my dick in thick spurts, covering the wall and then going down the drain. I sag against the wall of the shower, taking a moment to recover from my orgasm. I swear to Christ I've never cum harder than when I'm thinking about Nova - which is something I've been doing all the damn time since I first saw her. Yet, even as I come down from my high, I still feel unsatisfied. Hollow. Incomplete. I'll only ever know true pleasure when Isaiah and I get her into bed for real.

There's no doubt in my mind it will happen. The universe wouldn't put someone as perfect as Nova in our lives just to rip her away. No, she's going to get two big cowboys to take care of her in every single fucking way, even if she's trying to play hard to get. I know what I saw in those big, vulnerable, golden eyes of hers. She wants this too, but something is scaring her off.

I quickly finish cleaning myself up before the water goes cold, and then hop out and get dressed. Isaiah and I need to hit up the hardware store and a few other places this afternoon. Technically, it's my day off, but everyone has been working overtime lately. I don't mind. I love the people here and I'm happy to step up and fill in when necessary.

I pull the truck around to the stables where Isaiah has been working with a new horse. We all train the horses, but Isaiah is particularly good at it. Especially when it comes to unruly horses or timid horses. It's kind of fascinating to watch.

Too bad I don't have time for that today. We need to go into town, hit up the hardware store and the feed store, and then hightail it back here. The list of projects gets longer every day.

"Yo, Iz, you ready to go?" I call out to him. He nods and finishes up brushing Beauty, the most recent rescue horse, before heading my way.

Fifteen minutes later, we're pulling into the parking lot of McLeon's Hardware. Guess who's there in the parking lot trying to shove seven trees' worth of lumber into the back of that old rusted truck?

My kitten. Nova. The goddess of my dreams.

I barely have time to put the truck in park before I'm scrambling out of the cab. There's no way in hell I'm missing even one more second with Nova.

"Hey, where the hell are you go—"

Isaiah's question is cut off when he turns his head to see Nova battling with some chicken wire. I grin when I remember what he told me about his experience giving her a ride. Nova refused to give him her name. God, she's fucking perfect. Now I just need her number.

I make my way over to Nova, looking over my shoulder to make sure Isaiah is following me. He is. I don't even try to hide my smug smile.

Nova hasn't seen us yet, which gives me the chance to study her. She's every bit as mouth-watering as I remember. More so, even. Those curves, that ass... Jesus, she's got me half-hard already and she's not even doing anything.

But then I look up at her sweet face, which is a little pale, despite the physical labor she's doing. She's got dark circles under her eyes and the way she's holding herself lets me know she's about as bone tired as I am. I can't quite say what it does to me to see her this way.

I still very much want her sweet, soft body underneath me, above me, however she'll have me. But I also want to comfort her, hold her while she sleeps, and feed her breakfast in bed.

I take a second to let that feeling settle into my chest. I've never had these thoughts or urges with another woman, but it all makes sense when I look at her. I've always been one to roll with the punches, and Nova was a punch to the fucking gut from the moment I laid eyes on her.

"Hey there, beautiful," I say once I've come to terms with the fact that Nova is mine, *ours*, no matter what details we all still have to work out.

She freezes and slowly lifts her head up to meet my gaze. Nova's eyes are narrowed at me, but I see her fighting a smile. "My name is not beautiful," she mutters, going back to wrestling some chicken wire into the bed of the truck.

"What is your name, then?" Isaiah asks, shocking the hell out of me with his playful tone.

Nova's head pops up again as she stares down Isaiah. "Of *course*, both of you are here," she sighs, rolling her eyes. That smile is getting harder and harder to hide, which pleases me to no end. Nova gives me a questioning look. "You didn't tell him?"

"Nah. I told him he had to work for it," I say with a wink. Nova gives me a little grin that sets my whole world on fire.

"I'll work for it," Isaiah grunts, grabbing some lumber from the hand cart and hauling it into the truck.

"No, thanks. I've got everything covered here," she says, taking the two-by-four out of Isaiah's hands and placing it in the truck herself. I jump in and grab another bundle of chicken wire that's propped up against the wheel of the truck, easing it into the bed. "I said, *no, thank you*," Nova huffs.

I hold my hands up and back away, just as Isaiah grabs the third and final bundle of chicken wire, tossing it into the truck.

"Stop! Stop it right now, you goons!" Nova exclaims, making me chuckle. She has the cutest little scowl on her face as she puts her hands on her hips. "Stop helping me! I'm fine, I can do it—"

Just then, the pile of wood in the truck bed shifts, and Isaiah and I each grab one of her arms and pull her back right before several pieces of lumber come tumbling out and land right where her cute little feet were just a second earlier.

Nova stumbles backward into Isaiah's chest, and he wraps a protective arm around her waist. She gasps softly and squeezes her eyes shut, leaning into him a bit like she's savoring his touch. Interesting. She may have the tough girl act down, but there are these rare moments of vulnerability. She's so pure, so fucking beautiful, even as she fights with herself and her desire to be cherished, to be held, to be taken care of.

I want to kiss her soft lips and tell her she has nothing to worry about anymore, but I settle on tucking some of her silky auburn hair behind her ear. Nova pops her eyes open, hitting me with her defiance, her longing, her doubt.

"Good thing you had us goons to look out for you," I murmur, letting my fingers trail down her neck and circle her pulse point.

Isaiah draws little circles over her hip where his hand is resting. For a brief second, I think Nova is going to cry. My heart squeezes up painfully inside of my chest at the sight. But then the mask snaps into place, covering up her brokenness and bitterness with cool indifference. She shoves me away and steps out of Isaiah's embrace, even though I *know* it pains her to do it.

Keep denying us, beautiful. We won't give up on you.

"Thanks," she murmurs, stepping further away from us and wrapping her arms around herself. I don't think she's even aware she's doing it. Something about that tugs at my gut.

I look over and see Isaiah's normally indifferent face painted with worry. He's feeling the same thing. I knew he was as into her as I am, but I thought it would take longer for him to accept that fact. The way he's looking at Nova right now, though, I'd almost say he's half in love with her already.

"What are you building?" I ask, bending down to pick up a few of the things that fell out of the truck. Nova doesn't try to stop me this time.

"My mom has always wanted raised flower beds. Now that I'm back in town and it's my day off, it seemed like a good time to get started on them," she shrugs.

"Is that a good idea? You swinging a hammer around and all?" I tease her.

Her face turns slightly pink, but she smiles as she huffs out a breath.

"Do you need help building them?" Isaiah offers. I glance over at him as he stacks a few pieces of wood up and lifts them into the truck. We don't have time for another project with everything else going on, but Isaiah and I will work hard tomorrow to make up for it. If Nova wants our help, we'll be there.

I think Nova is going to shut him down, but to my surprise, she shrugs. That's practically a yes when it comes to my kitten.

"Do you know how to build a raised flower bed?" she asks, trying to keep her tone indifferent.

"Sure, we do stuff like that all the time on the ranch," I chime in.

"Hm," she nods thoughtfully, not quite agreeing to the offer, but not disagreeing either.

After a few moments of working in silence, it becomes clear that she won't be able to fit all of this stuff into the truck. Isaiah must notice this at the same time I do, because he gives me a slight nod, motioning towards our truck. I nod back in confirmation. Twin telepathy might not be real, but Isaiah and I can definitely communicate without words.

"Let's throw the rest of this stuff in our truck," I say, already grabbing one of the huge bags of mulch and heading that way. "Do you have wire cutters at home? And some rebars or stakes?" I ask, looking over my shoulder at Nova. I have to suppress my grin when I see her following me with some odds and ends she picked up.

"Uh..."

Isaiah steps in, clearly seeing where I'm going with this. "I'll swing by the ranch and get the rest of the stuff we'll need for your project," he states like it's already the plan.

"We, huh?" She graces us with a rare but breathtaking smile. That sliver of her true self she keeps hidden away makes everything worth it.

"Yup," I confirm. "You're stuck with us, kitten," I wink. She blushes and dips her face down so I don't see the effect my words had on her. I fight the urge to reach out and tip her chin up. I never want her to hide from me. From us. But she needs to feel safe, which means I have to try to keep my hands off her. For now.

We get everything loaded up and I look over at Isaiah, having another silent conversation. I know he understands once I start walking towards Nova's truck.

"I'll pick up the stuff we need for the ranch, drop it off, and then come by your house with the tools," he states. "What's your address, princess?"

Isaiah looks as shocked as I do at his term of endearment for her. It rolled off his tongue so easily. I'll have to give him shit about it later. How can I not? He really makes it too easy sometimes.

"Oh my *God*, not you, too!" Nova throws her hands up in exasperation. I think she likes our nicknames for her. I know I do.

Isaiah ticks his lips up in an almost smile. She's good for him. For us. I already know she's going to be an important part of our lives for a long time. Maybe even forever.

"What else am I supposed to call you when you refuse to give me your name?"

"You think I'll give you my address but not my name?" She scoffs, though it's not a very strong protest. There's no strength behind her words.

Isaiah shrugs but gives her another rare smile. "Do you want my help or not?" he asks gently. It's the same tone he uses when he's trying to earn the trust of the skittish horses. Even the angry, wild ones are skittish in their own way. At the end of the day, all of their anger stems from fear. Isaiah has this way about him that exudes peace and confidence when he's working with them. He might come across as a grumpy bastard, but he's got all the patience and gentleness in the world when it comes to things he cares about. That's how I know he's a goner for her already.

Nova stares at Isaiah, and then at me. Isaiah's question hangs in the air, unanswered. We all know he's talking about more than the raised garden beds. She furrows her brow and worries that juicy bottom lip of hers. I know Isaiah is staring at the motion as well.

After what feels like an eternity, Nova finally nods her head. "Yeah. Um, that would be... I mean, thanks. Are you sure you have the time?"

Definitely not, I think to myself. But that's no matter. If Nova wants us, she'll get us. She has no idea how much of us she's getting, but she will soon.

"For you, kitten? We'll always make time." I wink at her. She rolls her eyes, making Isaiah laugh. It's a little rusty, but damn is it good to know he's still capable of joy.

"And what about you? Does Jacob always speak on your behalf?" she asks saucily.

"Between the two of us, he got all of the communication skills," he answers.

"And what did you get?"

"The good looks, obviously," he deadpans. Shit, did he just *wink* at her?

Nova giggles, the beautiful sound lighter than air and brighter than sunshine.

"Come on, beautiful. Let's head over to your place. You can text Isaiah your address," I say, opening her door for her. She hops up into the truck, not even glaring at me for holding the door. Progress.

I give Isaiah a little smirk, knowing we're going to have her number now. It's a pretty brilliant move on my part, in my humble opinion.

When I get around to my side of the truck, I see Nova taking deep breaths and gripping the steering wheel. Is she really that nervous? She doesn't need to be. I wish I knew what she was thinking so I could ease her anxiety.

She snaps back into her normal self as soon as I open the door. "Ready, beautiful?" I ask. Nova glares at me, but there's no venom in her eyes, only playfulness.

That's it, my sweet Nova. You can trust us.

Chapter 5

Nova

I only agreed to their help because of my mom. Or so I tell myself. She's been talking about the raised flower beds for years, but she doesn't have the discipline or organizational skills to make it happen. I know she's tired of being all cooped up in the house, but she's not strong enough to run around town without me. I haven't had the time or energy to go on errands with her ever since starting my new job. Hopefully having a garden for her to work on will be an acceptable compromise.

I'm acutely aware of Jacob's presence in my truck. I swear I can feel the heat radiating off his body. His delicious, strong, muscled body that is probably carved out of stone or something. Ugh. Try as I might to dispel those thoughts, he's not making it easy. The man smells like sandalwood and saltwater. It's not fair. How can he be so perfect? And how can he have a freaking *twin* who is so different and yet equally as perfect? I'm still trying to wrap my head around it all.

"Where are you taking me, beautiful?" Jacob asks. "I'm pretty sure this is the perfect spot to dump a body," he jokes.

"If I wanted you dead, I would have finished off the job when I crashed into you," I shoot back. This makes Jacob laugh, the rich sound filling the cab and making my stomach flip. I even smile and laugh along with him. I can't help it. The way he laughs and gives of himself so easily makes me want to soak up whatever he has to offer and give it right back to him.

"Fair enough," he grins.

"I actually live in the next town over. Is that okay? I didn't even think about—"

"Of course, it's okay. Don't worry about a thing."

This makes me snort out a bitter laugh. "That's unlikely," I mutter to myself.

"Maybe before you met us," Jacob counters. Shoot. Apparently, I was louder than I thought.

I don't respond to him, because what do I say to that? Part of me wants to pull the car over, jump in his lap, and bury my face in his neck so I can smell him and touch him and ask him to live up to all of the kind things he's said to me since I've known him. But then I'm plagued with guilt that I want to do the same to Isaiah. I want them both to...to what? I don't even know. It's all too much.

The rest of the ride to my place is quiet, but not uncomfortably so. It's peaceful. Thoughtful, even. Jacob helps me unload everything once we get to the cottage and then directs me to organize the lumber by size.

"Tell me about you, Nova. What do you do?" he asks as we sort through the numerous piles of wood.

"I'm a waitress." My face heats with the admission of my new job title. It's not that I'm ashamed or that it's a bad job. It's just not where I thought I'd be. I wanted to study business, maybe be an accountant. I keep all the books for my mom's business and I've always liked numbers. They are constant. Never changing. Familiar. Reliable.

"Oh yeah?" Jacob perks up. "Where at?"

"Roy's Tavern."

"No shit? That's our favorite place to eat!"

"That's literally the *only* place to eat," I laugh.

"Both can be true."

I roll my eyes at him, but he just smiles at me like he knows I'm not really annoyed. "What do you do on the ranch?" I ask, not wanting to talk about my dead-end job or what brought me back here.

"A little bit of everything," he says, the pride evident in his voice. "Isaiah and I were hired on a few years ago at Rivera Ranch. It's hard work, but you'll never find better people to work with. The family has expanded over the last year. Our foreman got married to the new owner, and the cook got married to one of the ranch hands. Both of them recently had kids, so things are a bit rowdy, but I kind of like it that way," he smiles.

Jacob lifts the hem of his shirt up to wipe the sweat off his forehead. Good lord, that six-pack. So defined, so smooth, so tempting. I try to avert my eyes before he catches me, but I'm too late. He smirks and then continues telling me about Rivera Ranch.

"Honestly, coming to the ranch was the best thing that ever happened to Isaiah and me. We were both struggling after our parents died in a car accident, and finding a place where we belong, finding our people, saved us in more ways than one."

My breath catches in my throat at his words. He's being so open with me, a near stranger. I never would have guessed someone so carefree and happy has endured such pain.

Before I even realize what I'm doing, my hand reaches out and grasps Jacob's forearm. "I'm so sorry you lost your parents," I whisper. "That must have been awful. I don't know what I would do if..." My voice cracks, and to my horror, tears sting my eyes. I can't help but think about my mom and the fear of losing her. Yeah, the doctors say her odds of beating cancer are good, but it still scares the shit out of me every minute of every day.

I pull my hand back and turn around, unwilling to cry in front of this man who just bared his heart to me. I'm so selfish to be thinking about my own stuff while he's talking about his parents. God, what is wrong with me? I didn't even cry when my mom broke the news to me, and here I am, on the verge of tears for the second time today.

I take a few steps away to try and compose myself, but Jacob doesn't let me get too far. I feel the heat of his massive body behind me, and then his hands are on my hips, gently pulling me back into his chest. I want to cringe and twist away from him, knowing his hands are on my wide hips. It's always been a "problem area" for me, along with my belly pooch and thick thighs. I've never had anyone touch me there, or anywhere, really.

He feels so good though, so warm and sure of himself. Instead of backing off in disgust like I expect him to, Jacob grasps my soft flesh a little harder, like he can't get enough. I can't help but lean into his touch. Just like when Isaiah held me, my body seems to respond in a way it never has to anyone or anything before. I crave human connection on this level.

Jacob's hold on me is different than his brother's. Isaiah was surprisingly gentle, tentative even like he didn't want to scare me off. There's nothing tentative about the way Jacob is holding me now. He's sure and determined. Like I'm already his. I shiver slightly at that thought, but then shut it down quickly. How can I want them both so much?

"Don't hide from me, beautiful," Jacob whispers, placing the sweetest kiss on my temple. "I'm not scared of your tears or whatever put them in your eyes. Isaiah and I have known our fair share of suffering, but we're okay now, thanks to the support system we've found. Someday, I hope you trust us enough to be that for you."

I should say something or turn around or run far away from the feelings of need and longing he's bringing out in me, but before I have a chance to do anything, the front door swings open.

My mother is standing on the porch with a tray of lemonade and cookies. I rush over to her and take the tray, not wanting her to exert too much energy.

"I've got this, honeykins," she says, waving me away. "Even in my compromised state, I'm steadier on my feet than you," she laughs. Jacob joins her, so I glare at him over my shoulder. He just grins.

"I'm Jacob, ma'am," he says, striding over and taking the tray from her hand. She lets him. Traitor.

"Well, aren't you handsome," my mom fans herself with her hands, making me roll my eyes. Jacob is eating this right up, winking at me as if he knows something I don't. "I'm Miranda. How do you know my daughter?"

"I'm right here, you know," I mumble, crossing my arms over my chest like a petulant child.

I don't know why it bothers me so much that Jacob and my mother are getting along. Maybe because I know she won't stop talking about it for at least a month. I've never had a boyfriend. I didn't even go to prom, that's how much of a loser I was in high school. I've certainly never brought home a guy to meet my mom. Not that this is like that. Not at all.

"Of course you are, honeykins." My mom pats my arm patronizingly while still smiling at Jacob expectantly.

"Nova sort of...crashed into my life rather unexpectedly."

"Nova!" My mom turns to me. "Is this the man you hit with the truck?"

"How did you—"

"Just because I'm an invalid doesn't mean I didn't notice the smashed in hood or cracked windshield. I figured you'd handle it, so I didn't say anything."

Of course, I'll handle it. I always handle it, I think to myself.

Mom turns to Jacob and practically beams at him. I am already cringing at whatever she's going to say next. "What an adorable way for you two to meet. You know, my Nova here is always so responsible, but she's a bit accident-prone. She could use a man to watch out for her."

"Oh my God, mother, can you not?" I groan. I swear my cheeks are about to erupt in flames, I'm blushing so hard.

"I agree," Jacob says, chuckling. "I hope to do just that. If Nova lets me, of course."

"I hate to break it to you, but I think someone else is also hoping to take care of your girl."

"Mom, seriously?" I say incredulously. His girl?

"He looks a lot like you, too. Brothers, perhaps?"

What the hell is she talking about? How does she know about Isaiah? Maybe she does notice a lot more than I give her credit for.

"You must mean my twin, Isaiah. Is he here?"

"Out front, looking at the car."

She barely has time to get the words out of her mouth before I'm stomping around to the front of our house towards the driveway. Sure enough, Isaiah has the hood of the car pried open, which is no small feat considering how smashed up it is. He's bending over, inspecting something inside. I shove down the inappropriate thought of how good his ass looks in his jeans. Who even am I right now?

"Hey!" I shout, running over to him. "What do you think you're doing?"

Isaiah stands up and turns towards me, wiping his hands on an old rag. "Checking out the damage for myself. I don't know how you've been driving around this hunk of junk all week."

God, I know I just saw him an hour ago, but his green eyes somehow manage to catch me off guard. They are the same color as Jacob's, but different somehow. Jacob's are bright and full of comfort, but Isaiah's are deep and a little dark. Sharp. But just as brilliant and captivating.

"I, uh..." I stutter like an idiot. I clear my throat and try again. "I can't pay you for this."

Isaiah graces me with a smile. It's surprisingly warm and genuine and sends a tingle up my spine. I can tell he doesn't use it much, and something about him showing it to me has me feeling some kind of way.

"How about you tell me your name, princess?" he says softly so our growing audience of Jacob and my mom don't hear. I want to hate his little pet name for me, but my stupid stomach flutters and my heart squeezes up in my chest to hear the word fall from his lips.

I manage to shake these ridiculous thoughts from my head and turn to glare at Jacob. He puts his hands up in surrender. "I was not part of this. Isaiah did it all on his own, I just asked him to get tools for the raised flower beds."

"Well isn't that so sweet?" my mom says, laying it on thick. I roll my eyes and turn back to Isaiah, who has resumed working on the truck.

"You know, kitten, if you wanted to thank us, you could let us take you out for drinks tomorrow night," Jacob says, picking up on the not-so-subtle hints from my mother that she approves. He's going to play that up, I can already tell.

I'm about to turn him down when my mom opens her big mouth.

"Yes!" She claps her hands excitedly. "What a wonderful idea! She accepts. My honey bear deserves to relax after the crazy month she's had."

I huff out an annoyed breath, but if I'm being honest with myself, I'm kind of glad my mom spoke up. There's no way I'd have agreed to go out so easily, but now I have an excuse.

"Excellent. It's settled then," Jacob says, that stupidly sexy, confident grin taking over his face and making him impossibly more attractive.

I roll my eyes at him for good measure.

"Now that that's all settled, I better get inside and lie down. I'm a bit tired."

I'm by her side in a second, taking her arm. "Are you feeling okay? Any nausea? Pain? Headaches?"

"Just tired. I can manage to put myself to bed. You should stay out here with your guests," she winks at me. It's then I realize she's not tired at all, which fills me with equal parts relief and annoyance that she's manipulating me.

"Let me help you, Miranda," Jacob says easily. My mom smiles up at him, clearly planning our wedding in her head and picturing what our children will look like.

They head inside, leaving me alone with Isaiah.

"Are you going to tell me your name?" he asks while still tinkering under the hood. "I'm working real hard here," he adds.

"No, but I bet you're just going to go inside and ask my mom," I mutter.

Isaiah stands up again and turns towards me. He takes a step closer, and for some reason, I don't back away. He's right in front of me, close enough for me to take in his earthy scent with a hint of pine. "Easy, now, sweet girl," he says so softly, so gently I almost don't recognize his voice. "I'll never take something you don't freely give."

My breath catches in my throat as I look up at him. There's a genuineness to his words, a conviction beyond anything I've ever experienced. It has me trusting him, just a little. Just enough.

"Nova," I whisper, dipping my head down to stare at my feet. This moment feels oddly intimate, though I don't know why. I just told him my name. It's not a big deal. Why then do I feel like this somehow changes everything?

"Nova," he repeats, matching my quiet tone. One calloused finger touches my chin, tipping it up to look at him again. "Thank you."

I furrow my brow, not sure why he's thanking me, but then Jacob comes bounding towards us, a ball of excited energy.

"We've got mom's approval, *honeykins*."

I take a step back from Isaiah and turn my attention towards Jacob, thankful for the comedic relief from the intense moment Isaiah and I were sharing. I groan at his use of my mom's name for me. "It seems as though I'm a magnet for embarrassing nicknames."

"I think you like it, kitten. You may be all claws and indifference on the outside, but I think you secretly want to be all cuddly and warm and fuzzy."

I shrug and start walking away from both of them, towards the unfinished flower beds in the backyard. "Think whatever you want. Just because you won my mom over doesn't mean you'll get my approval so easily."

Jacob loops an arm around my waist as I'm walking past him, pulling my back to his front. Just like last time, I find my body betraying me and melting into his embrace. "That's alright, beautiful. I've always liked a challenge. You're worth the chase."

I don't know what to say to that, so I wiggle my way out of his arms, ignoring the cold, empty feeling that washes over me. Good lord, I don't think I'll survive a date with these two. Not that it's a date. Just drinks.

Yeah, keep telling yourself that.

Chapter 6

Nova

"Are you ready for your date, honey bun?" my mom calls from the living room.

"For the hundredth time, it's *not* a date!" I shout back. Even as I say the words, my hands shake with anticipation as I look at myself in front of the mirror. If it's not a date, then why am I so nervous? Why did I take time to curl my hair and dig in my closet to find something other than jeans and a t-shirt?

I walk into the living room just in time to hear my mom mutter, "Whatever you need to tell yourself to get out the front door," under her breath.

I ignore her comment and instead grab my mom's water bottle to fill it up. I fill up a tray with cookies, grapes, a few apple slices, and some cheese and bring everything out to her.

"Nova, you really didn't have to bring me all of this," she says around a mouthful of cookie. I grin and shake my head. There's a reason I only put two on there. I swear the woman is half cookie. How she's always been a size six is beyond me.

"Make sure to eat some fruit, too," I say, turning the tray so the grapes are closer to her reach than the other cookie.

"Yes, *mom*," she says dramatically, giving me a wink. "Now come here and let me see my beautiful daughter. It's not every day you go on your first date."

"Not a date," I remind her. "Drinks. With...friends, I guess. I don't really know what to call a guy I hit with my truck and then brought back here to do manual labor."

"And don't forget is twin brother," my mother so helpfully adds.

"Right. I don't know what to call him either. Collateral damage?"

"How about you call them sweet? Perfect? Super hot and sex—"

"Enough!" I cut her off, putting my hand in the air to emphasize my point.

"Okay, okay, I'm done. But it's okay to let someone in, you know. You've kept your heart locked up so tight, always such a responsible woman, even when you were a little kid. I swear you didn't have a childhood, despite my best efforts."

"I thought you said you were done," I mutter. Mom shakes her head and sighs dramatically right before the doorbell rings.

"Go on, don't leave those handsome men waiting!" Mom shoos me off.

I head for the front door and take a calming breath before opening it. Good god, these two are stunning. Both of them are in dark, fitted jeans that are slung low on their hips. Isaiah has on a black t-shirt that shows off his muscled arms. I never noticed his full sleeves of tattoos before, since he's worn long-sleeved flannels both times I've seen him. Jacob is in a forest green Henley that molds around his defined muscles and makes my mouth water. And did I mention that they *both* have a bouquet of flowers?

"Kitten, you look amazing," Jacob says, leaning in to kiss my cheek. I don't mean to close my eyes and breathe in his sandalwood smell. Really, I don't. "These are for Miranda, is she home?"

"Right in here, sweetie!" Mom calls out.

"Suck up," I tease, trying to hide my smile at the clear affection my mom and Jacob already have for one another. He laughs and gives me another kiss on my forehead before striding into the living room like he owns the place. I turn my attention towards Isaiah, who is still standing on the porch, staring at me.

"Are those for me?" I ask after a moment of silence stretches between us. Isaiah nods his head slowly, his eyes roaming up and down my body. I've never felt so on display, so vulnerable, so...desirable.

"Yeah," he clears his throat, snapping his eyes up to meet mine. "Yes. These are for you," he repeats.

Isaiah steps closer and kisses me on the cheek as well, but he keeps his face close to mine, nuzzling his nose right below my ear. Is this really happening? Am I going on a date with *two* big, chiseled, sinfully hot cowboys? I mean, they brought flowers and kissed me.

"God, you smell good," he whispers, more to himself than to me.

"Th-thank you," I stammer once Isaiah pulls away from me. I'm not sure if I'm thanking him for his oddly sweet and intimate gesture, the compliment, or the flowers. "Come in, I have to find vases for these."

I turn around and walk into the house, leading Isaiah into the kitchen where Jacob is digging around in the cupboards for something. Seeing him make himself right at home brings a smile to my face before I can stop it.

"Kitten!" Jacob exclaims like we've been separated for weeks, not just a few minutes. I won't lie, his excitement makes me feel all warm and fuzzy inside. Just like he said yesterday. "Where are the cookies? Your mom said she stashed some Girl Scout cookies in here."

"I'm not even surprised," I laugh. "I'm guessing they are on the top shelf? Maybe behind her sugary cereals? I can't reach that high."

"Ah, there they are. Miranda is a tricky one, isn't she?"

"You have no idea," I sigh. Isaiah walks over to the China hutch and opens one of the lower cabinet doors. "What are you looking for?" I asked, confused.

He doesn't answer. Instead, he shuffles some stuff around and then turns back towards me, holding two vases. It's such a small thing, but it has me feeling all warm and fuzzy again. I said I needed vases, and he went and found some.

Jacob winks at me and gives me a big smile as he heads back out to the living room. I swear he can read my freaking mind and he's pretty pleased with the thoughts he and his twin are inspiring.

Isaiah and I fill the vases with water and arrange the flowers. I leave one bouquet on the table and tell Isaiah we can leave one on the coffee table in the living room. When we get out there, Jacob is chowing down on grapes and cheese while my mom is already a third of the way through a sleeve of Thin Mints.

"Hey, leave some fruit for my mom, she needs to have something other than cookies!"

"I had a grape," mom informs me. "I just needed a palate cleanser before having some cheese."

"Yeah, I saw her. She totally had a grape. Maybe even two," Jacob nods.

"You're just as bad as she is," I shake my head in mock disappointment.

"Ready to go?" Isaiah asks from behind me. I nod and Jacob pops one last grape into his mouth before grabbing my hand and leading us towards the front door.

"Goodbye, Miranda!" Jacob says over his shoulder.

"Have fun, you three. Don't do anything I wouldn't do!"

"Oh my God," I groan.

Jacob just laughs, ushering us outside. Isaiah even chuckles, the deep sound rumbling out of his chest, making me feel tingly between my legs. How am I this turned on already? And more importantly, how am I going to survive the entire evening with these two without melting into a puddle or bursting into flames or doing something completely crazy and giving them my virginity?

Stop it! I chastise myself.

Isaiah gets in on the driver's side while Jacob opens the passenger door and helps me up, climbing in after me. It's a tight fit for all three of us, but I'm not complaining. Jacob throws his arm over my shoulder, encouraging me to lean against his chest. And what a chest it is. Good lord. I close my eyes and breathe him in, savoring this moment of closeness.

My eyes snap open when I feel Isaiah's hand rest on top of mine. He gives me an adorably shy look like he's not quite sure if it's okay for him to be touching me like this. I mean, I have no idea what the rules are, but if both of them want to touch me then hell yes, I'm in. I turn my hand over and lace our fingers together, giving his hand a squeeze.

Isaiah's lips spread into a full-on smile, radiating warmth and satisfaction. I feel the intensity of it deep in my chest. That feeling is magnified when Jacob presses his lips to the top of my head. These two. What am I going to do with them? No, seriously. What the hell is going to happen between the three of us?

We ride in silence for a while, though not uncomfortably so. In fact, everything about Jacob and Isaiah feels...right. Like we fit, somehow. The three of us belong together.

"What are you thinking about?" Jacob murmurs.

I feel my cheeks heat up at his question. There's no way I'm telling him my actual thoughts. The idea of the three of us...what, being in a relationship? It's completely insane.

"Nothing," I say all too quickly.

"Whatever it wass must have been a happy thought. You sighed so sweetly just now."

"I did?" I whisper, tilting my head up and getting lost in his green eyes. Where are all of my defenses? Where are the walls I always try to keep in place?

"You did," Jacob confirms. "You can keep your secrets, for now, kitten, but we're going to know all of you soon enough."

"Slow down, Jacob. We haven't even bought her a drink yet," Isaiah grumbles on the other side of me.

Jacob shoots him a glare but then returns his attention to me, giving me a playful wink. "Of course. All in good time."

Isaiah pulls the truck into the parking lot of Roy's Tavern, which makes me laugh.

"I know, I know, it's totally lame to take you to your place of work for a drink, but the only other option was taking you back to our place, and we thought it might be too soon for that," Jacob explains. I nod.

"See? Look at me pacing myself and all that. I'm quite the gentleman," he says with a grin. Isaiah grunts something, making me laugh again.

Once inside, I nod my head at Paul, the bartender, and wave at a few of my other co-workers. It's not unusual to see employees here when they are off the clock. This is the only dining establishment around for miles, after all.

Jacob grabs drinks for us while Isaiah and I find an empty booth. I slide in on one side, assuming Isaiah will sit across from me. Instead, he scoots right up next to me, throwing his arm over the back of the booth casually. I can feel the heat of his thigh where it lightly touches mine.

I almost jump out of my seat when his thumb softly strokes the side of my neck. Looking up at the solid wall of tattooed muscle sitting next to me, I see he's staring straight ahead, wearing a slight grin on his handsome face. Isaiah slowly turns towards me, his eyes deep and dark, yet gentle, somehow.

"This okay, sweet girl?" he whispers, still gliding his thumb along the side of my neck, stopping briefly to circle a super-sensitive spot behind my ear. It's the same low, soft tone he used with me yesterday when he said he would never take anything that I didn't freely give.

"Yeah," I nod. "I like it. I mean..." God, why am I such a spaz? "Uh, I mean it feels good."

Oh my God, seriously, Nova?

Isaiah chuckles, the gravelly sound resonating from deep within his chest. "I like making you feel good," he murmurs into the shell of my ear, his lips barely touching me. My heart is beating rapidly in my chest, the frantic rhythm mirrored between my legs.

"You two got cozy awfully quickly," Jacob chides playfully, setting our drinks down.

He looks at the seat Isaiah and I are sharing, and then at the empty seat across from us. I can practically see him trying to figure out a way to fit all three of us on the same side, but eventually, Jacob plops down across from us. He immediately reaches out for my hand, rubbing his calloused thumb across the back of my knuckles so sweetly. These tender touches are going to be my downfall, I can already feel it.

"So, kitten, tell us everything about you," Jacob says.

"Like what?"

Jacob grins at me. I've never understood how a grin could be "panty-melting," but I do now. "Tell me what CD you were listening to when you ran into me."

"I can't give away all my secrets on the first date." I grin back at him.

"The rap music?" Isaiah asks. Well, shoot.

Jacob's eyebrows practically disappear into his hairline. "Like Drake and Eminem?"

I shake my head no, but then sigh when I realize he's not going to let this go. "More like Tupac and Biggie."

Jacob laughs, and Isaiah's lips tip up into a smile. I suppose the confession was worth it to see them happy.

Reel it in, girl!

"So, anyway, other than that, I'm pretty boring. I live with my mom, I work here, and I'm a little accident-prone," I shrug, taking a sip of my drink.

"First of all, old school hip-hop? I will definitely be circling around to that later, kitten. Second, there's nothing boring about you. You're a fucking knock-out, you're feisty as hell, you're willing to put up with our shit, and your mom is a hippy who is into the healing powers of crystals and cookies."

"Oh no, did she try to sell you one of her magic healing bracelets?" I groan.

"No way," he shakes his head emphatically. I sigh in relief. "She sold me a green aventurine bolo tie."

"Noooo!" I laugh. "And you bought it?"

"Hell yeah, I did! Miranda said it matches my eyes," Jacob says, batting his long eyelashes at me dramatically.

"I hate to break it to you, but I think she had an alternative agenda."

"Miranda? Scheming? I don't believe it!" Jacob gasps, throwing his hand over his heart.

Isaiah barks out a laugh, making me smile.

"Believe it. Green aventurine is for your heart chakra. Mother dearest likes to think of herself as a bit of a matchmaker."

"Oh, so *that's* what she was getting at when she—"

"Nova? Is that you?" Someone slurs from a few feet away.

All three of us turn our heads towards the direction of the voice. The area we're sitting in is dimly lit, so the man's facial features are obscured, but I'd know that voice anywhere. My face flushes and I grow tense. Isaiah instinctively holds me closer to him, sensing my distress. It's another small gesture that means so much to me.

"Y-yeah," I stutter out.

"Well, shee-it, girl. It's only been a year, but hot damn." He whistles at me, making my skin crawl. "What's going on here?" Tim nods his head towards Jacob and Isaiah, both still touching me in some way.

I'm about to answer when Isaiah cuts me off. "Who the hell are you?"

Tim jerks his head back, staring at Isaiah and then at me like I'm going to come to his rescue or something. "Nova and I were friends in high school. I didn't know she was back. Sheesh."

Isaiah glares at him, right along with Jacob. Tim takes a hint and gives me a half-hearted wave before stumbling away.

"You dated that douche canoe in high school?" Jacob asks.

I choke on my drink, nearly spitting it out as I laugh at the ridiculous question. "No, definitely not. We weren't friends. Like, not at all. Tim was kind of a bully."

"He bullied you?" Isaiah grits out.

I shrug and take another sip of my drink, hoping to appear nonchalant about it. "He bullied everyone."

Isaiah growls, making me smile a bit. I rest my head on his shoulder, which seems to calm him down. "I don't think he'll be a problem anymore. I'm pretty sure Tim peed his pants when you yelled at him," I tease.

Jacob snickers, but Isaiah doesn't seem convinced.

"Anyway," I'm quick to move the conversation along. "Tell me about you guys. Twins, huh? That must have been fun growing up." I mentally kick myself for being so lame, but I'll take whatever out I can get when it comes to reliving my high school days.

Jacob takes pity on me and launches into story after story about him and Isaiah as kids. We laugh and joke around, even getting Isaiah to share a funny memory or two. Jacob and Isaiah tell me about working on the ranch, about the new babies and growing families, and how they truly love their work.

As the night goes on, I find myself drawn even more to them. I want to fit into their lives. I want to be a part of their family too. I want to be friends with Jade and Teagan and have my kids grow up with theirs.

Try as I might to shove that errant thought away, it keeps popping back up. Not only are Jacob and Isaiah these perfect male specimens with golden tan skin, lean, rippling muscles, bright green eyes, and strong, sharp facial features, but they are kind. Dependable. Family men. I find my heart melting right along with my panties.

Before I realize it, three hours have gone by. I try to hide a yawn, but it slips out anyway.

"You tired of us already?" Jacob teases.

"No, definitely not. But I am tired. I'm not used to the long hours and being on my feet all damn day," I admit, yawning again.

"Let's get you home before you turn into a pumpkin," Jacob says.

After closing out our tab, which only consisted of the three drinks we ordered when we first walked in, Jacob, Isaiah, and I head outside.

The air is thick with some kind of energy I've never felt before. It coats my skin in goosebumps and sends awareness to my aching center and sensitive nipples. My panties are ruined, thanks to being in the vicinity of my twin cowboys, but are they feeling what I'm feeling? How does this evening end? Where do we go from here? What—

Before I can finish that thought, Jacob spins me around and crashes his lips down on mine, walking me backward until we're hidden behind the truck. It's so surprising, so sudden, so overwhelmingly delicious, I gasp into his mouth. He groans and slips his tongue in between my lips, tasting me and treasuring me and turning me on even more.

His fingers tangle in my hair and angle my head to the side so he can deepen our kiss. I'm lost in the way his tongue caresses mine, the minty taste of his kiss, the way his breathing is shallow like mine. The kiss lasts for so long I think I might pass out from lack of oxygen.

Suddenly, Jacob rips his mouth away from mine and turns me around again, giving me a light push into Isaiah's arms. I barely have time to suck in fresh air before Isaiah kisses me as well. His lips are soft, his kiss gentle. It's unexpected but perfect.

Jacob was wild and untamed, taking me, claiming me, letting me know beyond a shadow of a doubt he wants me. Isaiah is more cautious, taking his time to explore me, giving me long, languid strokes of his tongue that make me roll my body against his.

He grunts and spears his fingers into my hair gripping the strands and holding me in place while his kisses turn more desperate.

Once again, I'm spun around, fast enough that I stumble a bit. Isaiah's hands grip my hips to steady me, pulling me back so my ass is brushing up against his very obvious erection. Jacob smirks, cupping my cheek in one massive hand while brushing a few strands of my hair away with the other.

"Do you have any idea how stunning you are?" Jacob whispers into my lips before kissing me again, softly this time. Isaiah plants kisses up and down my neck, making me melt against him, even as I grip Jacob's shirt to pull him closer.

God, having both of their warm, chiseled bodies pressed against mine, surrounding me with their strength, their touch... It's perfect.

Absolutely perfect. I can't believe they want me like this, but the way they are touching me, caressing me, kissing me, and worshipping my curves, leaves no room for doubt.

Jacob's hands roam down my body, cupping my breasts and kneading them gently. I instinctively bow my back, thrusting my breasts further into his hands.

"Does that feel good, beautiful? You like when I play with your amazing tits?" Jacob murmurs, kissing down the other side of my neck while Isaiah slides his hands from my hips to the hem of my dress.

"God yes, everything..." I gasp when I feel Isaiah's fingers skim up the inside of my thighs, up and down, lightly touching me, teasing me, driving me wild. "Everything feels so good," I finish, my voice a breathy whisper.

Isaiah's hand rubs the thin fabric of my panties, making my breath hitch. "Mmm," Isaiah growls behind me. "Fuck, princess, this pussy is begging for attention, isn't it?"

I whimper and jerk my hips into his touch, practically humping his hand. I don't even care anymore, I'm so lost in this, in them, in us. "Please," I whisper, trying to control my voice. I don't even know what I'm asking for, but Jacob and Isaiah do.

Isaiah continues to slide his fingers up and down my panty-covered slit, just that small touch setting me on edge. When his hand is joined by Jacob's, I can't hold back the moan. Isaiah pushes my panties aside while Jacob slips his finger into my soaking wet slit. We all groan at what is happening between us.

"God fucking damn, kitten," Jacob rasps out, circling my clit with his fingers. I squeeze my eyes shut and throw my head back so I'm resting on Isaiah's shoulder.

Isaiah turns his head and nuzzles into me, another oddly sweet gesture from the big, bad, tattooed cowboy, especially considering the dirty things that are happening right now. "Tell us if this is too much," he whispers, his hands trailing up from my thighs to where the waistline of my panties is, teasing me slightly by dipping his fingers inside.

I instinctively suck in my gut, but Isaiah spreads his massive hand over my belly and pulls me closer to him, nipping at the shell of my ear. "This thick, juicy body is perfect for us, princess. Don't hide, not from us."

My breath hitches at his words and I swallow down tears. Jacob said the same thing yesterday in my yard - *Don't hide from me.* Those words hit me deep. I'm so wrapped up in what is happening, I almost miss the fact that Jacob rips my panties right off me. I squeal, but he captures the sound with a punishing kiss.

"Hey!" I whisper-shout once we break apart. "I liked those panties!"

Jacob just grins and kisses me again while Isaiah slides one finger in and out of my tight channel. I gasp at the invasion, twitching in their arms. "I bet you'll like this more," Jacob whispers, replacing Isaiah's hand with his own.

He's right. I like their touch, their attention, their *everything* more than I like my panties. More than I like anything, really, and that should scare me. However, I don't have time to be scared when I have two mouths kissing my neck, my face, my chest, anywhere they can. I don't have time for doubts when four hands are touching me, massaging me, and bringing me more pleasure than I've ever known.

I've lost track of who is touching me where. All I know is that I'm being stretched and stroked by two gorgeous men who can't seem to get enough of me.

I don't want them to stop, though. I want whatever they have to give me, for however long they are willing to give it.

"Oh God," I gasp when I feel a finger circling my ass hole.

"Anyone ever touch you here, princess?" Isaiah asks, his voice tight with need.

I shake my head no and press back into him, making him groan. I hardly recognize this wanton woman I've become, but I can't say I don't like it. Jacob and Isaiah give me such confidence, how could I not give myself over to this unquenchable lust?

"Fucking hell, kitten, you're going to be the death of us," Jacob whispers before kissing me again.

Suddenly, there's one finger in my ass and one in my pussy, thrusting in and out, filling me fuller than I've ever been before. "Wh-what? Oh! Ohmygod, Ohmy*god*, please don't stop…"

We're all sharing short, ragged breaths as the loud, wet, smacking noises fill the air around us. My nerves sizzle and pop, my legs tremble, and I feel like I'm going to pass out from the overwhelming sensations taking over my body. I wrap an arm around Jacob's neck and then reach behind me and wrap my other arm around Isaiah, needing both of them to hold me up, to anchor me at this moment.

"That's it, princess, shit, I feel it, I feel you," Isaiah grunts, nipping my ear and shoving two fingers up my ass.

"So tight, so fucking wet, this pussy loves having two men giving it attention, isn't that right, kitten?"

I whimper and nod, gasping for air and clenching down on both of their fingers as they enter me again and again.

Jacob rests his forehead on mine, and I'm shocked to feel him trembling too. "Let go, Nova," he whispers. "Let go of every-fucking-thing and cum for us."

"I… I…"

"We've got you, princess. Trust us," Isaiah says, his deep voice like liquid comfort as he fingerfucks my ass.

The moment is so filthy, so tender, so vulnerable, I have no other choice but to surrender to them completely.

My muscles tense and lock up, my breath catches in my throat, and the intense knot of pressure low in my belly begins to throb outward until it consumes my entire being. I'm suspended in the air for a flash of a second, and then the world comes crashing down around me as I writhe and spasm around their fingers.

Jacob swallows my scream as he continues rubbing circles around my clit. Isaiah moves his hands to my breasts, squeezing them roughly and dry fucking me from behind, rubbing his obscenely hard cock against my ass as I buck against him.

"That's so fucking it," Isaiah grunts.

I gasp for air and deflate completely, the last of my orgasm dripping out of me and leaving me boneless. The last thing I see before letting my heavy eyelids close is Jacob licking my release off his long fingers.

I'm surrounded by my two strong men, each holding me up, pressing light kisses on my head, my face, my shoulders, wherever they can reach. Four hands soothe me, gently bringing me back down. They are treating me like I'm precious, like I just did them a favor instead of the other way around.

"You okay, kitten?" Jacob asks, tilting my head up and staring into my eyes.

"Y-yeah," I nod.

"Was that too much?" Isaiah asks, cupping my cheek and turning my head so we're eye to eye.

"It was perfect," I sigh. Isaiah grins at me, which lights me up from the inside out. I think I'd do just about anything to put a smile on his usually somber face. "Do you, um... I mean can I...?"

I don't even really know what I'm asking, let alone how to follow through on anything. They gave me an incredible orgasm, so I should give them each one too, right? Nothing in life is free, after all.

"Nope," Jacob says, kissing me on the cheek and stepping away from me.

"This was about you, sweet girl," Isaiah murmurs so only I can hear.

"But..." I start to protest.

"Let's get you back to Miranda. She's probably out of cookies by now," Jacob calls out from where he's sitting in the driver's seat.

Isaiah gently moves me aside so he can open up the door. "After you, princess," he says, crawling in after me and tucking me into his side.

Jacob places a hand on my thigh as soon as we're on the road. I feel so safe, so protected right here in between my men. Are they my men? What just happened?

"You still okay?" Isaiah asks in that peaceful, low tone of his that instantly puts me at ease.

"I am now," I sigh, snuggling up closer to him. He holds me the rest of the way to my house and gives me a kiss at my doorstep before stepping back to let Jacob kiss me as well.

I already can't wait to see them again. For the first time, maybe in my whole life, I'm excited for whatever lies ahead. Even if I have no idea what we're all doing.

Chapter 7

"What the fuck are we doing?" I demand as soon as Jacob and I get back into our cabin on the ranch.

"What do you mean?"

"What do I... Jesus, I'm talking about Nova," I practically roar, wiping my hands down my face in an attempt to chill out.

"Well, we took her out, kissed the hell out of her, fingered her in the parking lot, watched her cum like a fucking goddess, and then took her home," he says with a shrug. Bastard.

"Exactly. We took her home, not to our place. I thought you wanted to fuck her, not catch feelings for her," I grit out. Jacob bristles at my harsh words.

"Don't talk about her that way," Jacob snaps, stomping towards me. My eyebrows shoot up and I instinctively take a step back. Jacob never loses his cool like this. "I know you're bitter and broken, but I didn't think you were blind, too. Nova is perfect. I thought you felt it too. No, fuck that, I *know* you felt it."

I scoff at him, turning around so he can't see how accurate his statement really is. I know I'm being an asshole, but it's the only weapon I have against the vulnerability I'm feeling right now. I want her back here, but not so we can sleep with her. I want to hold her, make sure she's really okay, that we didn't push her too far. I had my hands on Nova in some way or another for the last four hours, and I want more of that. I feel disturbingly cold and empty without her here. I can't give in to those desires though.

"Since when do you think of women as perfect? I thought you wanted to be a bachelor for life?" I try to redirect the conversation to his shortcomings instead of my own.

"That was until I met Nova. To be fair, I didn't know she was perfect until I just...knew."

I spin around and scowl at him. "That makes no sense," I grumble, even though it does. I get it. I didn't know Nova was going to have the power to break me until she just...did. One minute I was standing on her front porch feeling like a chump with a bouquet of flowers in my hand, and the next minute I was giving her my goddamn heart.

"Bullshit. I know you. I know what it's like to share a woman with you, and never, *ever*, have you handled anyone with as much care, nor as much passion as when you were with Nova."

"That's because she's not the kind of girl who does this!"

"And what kind of girl is that, exactly?"

"Oh shove it. I'm not talking about slut-shaming. I'm just saying she's different. She'll want more than a one-night stand."

"Exactly. Which is why we're going to give her more than one night," Jacob smiles triumphantly. Dickhead.

I grunt, which only makes him chuckle.

"I don't know if I have anything more than that to give. In fact, I think I've already given too much," I mutter.

"Do you trust me, Isaiah?"

I snap my head up to look at my twin. "What do you mean?"

"It's a pretty simple question. Do you trust me?"

"Yeah. You know I trust you. I think you're the only person I trust in this whole world."

"Exactly. Trust me when I say Nova isn't Trish. She's not capable of betrayal like that. I know you know that too, deep down, but you're letting your insecurities talk right now. I gotta say, your insecurities are making you sound like a total bag of dicks."

I swipe a book off of the side table and throw it at him. Jacob dodges it easily, grinning the whole time.

"You've never been in love, so you don't know what it feels like to be heartbroken. I don't love Trish anymore, but that doesn't mean I'm eager to subject myself to more pain."

"Psssh, you were never in love with Trish," Jacob scoffs.

"The fuck you talking about? I was going to marry her!"

"And? So what? Lots of people get married who aren't in love. Lots of people *stay* married who aren't in love. Lots of people go their whole lives blissfully ignorant of how not in love they are."

I rub my temples in an attempt to ward off the incoming migraine. "What's your point?"

"My point is that you weren't in love with Trish. You were comfortable with her. I think your real issue is not trusting yourself."

"Whatever."

"No, not whatever. You know I'm right. Be honest with me, Isaiah. Fucking *look* at me."

I stop what I'm doing at stare right at him. He's never this intense, that's usually my thing.

"Now tell me you felt even *half* of what you do for Nova when you were with Trish. I'll know if you're lying. Go on. Tell me."

I grit my teeth and think about Trish. We were together for nearly two years, surely I still have deep feelings for her. Even anger, right? The woman broke my heart, I should be pissed at her. Instead, when I think of her, all I feel is relief that we're not together. When I think l of myself and our breakup, however, I feel fear. Fear that I wasn't enough, and that anyone who I open up to will find whatever I was lacking, and cheat on me too.

"Fuck you, Jacob," I spit out, hating how weak and vulnerable his stupid thought exercise is making me. "Even if I didn't love Trish, doesn't mean I want anything to do with Nova." I almost choke on the words, but I had to get them out.

Jacob starts laughing. And not just a little bit. The little shit is belly laughing and wiping his eyes. I grab another book and throw it at him, this time hitting him square in the chest. Good.

"Hey," he sputters out, rubbing his chest and still laughing. "I'm sorry, but that's the worst lie anyone has ever told in the history of the world." I lift an eyebrow at him, letting him know his hyperbole is not appreciated. "Dude, it's obvious you care about her. I mean, *princess?* Come on, you didn't give Trish a pet name. You've never given anyone a pet name, not even something generic like *baby.*"

I grunt in acknowledgment. Yeah, the whole *princess* thing just sort of happened. No one else has ever triggered the need for a cutesy name like that. I could lie to myself and say I only did it because I knew she would hate it, but then how would I explain why I call her *sweet girl?* That one scares me more than anything. When it's just me and her, and I can feel her tense up or get defensive, it's like I...I...I want to be the one to calm her down. I want to be her peace, her safety. I want to be the one she can be sweet with, be herself with.

"Fuck," I mutter more to myself than to Jacob. I look up, expecting him to have a smug grin on his face, but instead, I see understanding.

"Yeah. Fuck." We stand in silence for a few moments while the weight of what's happening sets in. We've only just met Nova, and yet she's changed us. I ache, though I don't know if it's for more of Nova or if it's because I'm preparing for the inevitable heartbreak.

"What now?" I ask. "We both...feel...*things* for her. How does that even work?"

Jacob rolls his eyes at me. "How do you think it works? We both share her. Forever." Jacob shrugs as if it's a done deal.

I choke on a cough, glaring at him when he laughs at me. "What the hell do you mean?"

"We. Both. Share. H—"

"Yes, I heard you, you idiot. But forever? A relationship? What would that even look like?"

"Were you jealous at all tonight? Or when we were helping her with her yard or the car?"

"No..."

"Right, me either. I knew when Nova needed to laugh, when she needed me to distract her mom, when she needed to be teased. You knew when she needed to be held, when she needed a calming presence, when she needed a gentle touch. And we both know she's incredibly strong, but that she needs someone to take care of her. So, why not us?"

"We've hardly spent more than a handful of hours with her. Life is going to get a lot more complicated than helping with household chores and taking her out for drinks."

"Yes and no," he says easily while digging through the fridge for something. God, he's so infuriating. More so when he makes sense and shuts down all my protests. "Life will certainly get more complicated, but our priorities won't. She's my priority. Everything else will fall in line. Or it won't. Either way, at the end of the day, I know I'll be content if we're all family."

"Goddamnit," I sigh, running my hands through my hair.

Jacob chuckles, handing me a beer. "So we're in agreement? Nova is ours?"

"What if I mess it up?"

"Don't."

"What if she chooses just one of us?"

"Not gonna happen."

"What if she chea—"

"Stop right there. Do not accuse our Nova of doing something like that."

"*Our* Nova, huh?"

"That's what I've been telling you!" Jacob says in exasperation.

This elicits a chuckle from me. "Our Nova," I say again, letting the words sink down into me this time, branding me with their warmth and ownership.

"Our nova," Jacob repeats, nodding his head. "God, how fucking incredible was she tonight? Her lips, her tongue, Jesus, her tight, hot pussy…" He groans and adjusts himself. Fuck, I have to do the same.

"I know. So damn responsive. I could tell when she finally trusted us, you know? Felt her body give up the fight and give in to her orgasm."

"And what an orgasm, shit. Can you imagine what it's going to be like to be inside of her when she cums like that? I can't wait to be buried in her juicy cunt while you fuck that tight ass."

That. Ass. Fuck me, that ass. Perfect, round, biteable. The way she pushed herself further onto my finger, practically begging me to fuck her tight little hole. And when she came? Jesus Christ, her walls sucked me in, pulsed and throbbed wildly while Jacob finished her off. I growl and slam my beer bottle on the table. "I'm taking a shower," I grunt. Jacob snickers at me, but he's just as hard as I am.

"Soon Nova will be here to join you!" he shouts over his shoulder. The thought of showering with Nova almost has me bursting in my goddamn jeans. She's going to be the death of me, one way or another.

***

"What time is it?" Jacob asks for the fifth time in as many minutes.

"Six-fifteen, same as last time you asked," I grumble while tidying up the living room of our small cabin out on the ranch.

"Well *excuse me* for wanting everything to be perfect for our girl," he scoffs.

I can't help the small smile that creeps into my features. *Our girl.* It's been a week since Jacob and I had our come to Jesus moment and he knocked some sense into me. If I didn't already know I was a goner for her, going seven days without seeing Nova would have done it.

We talked on the phone a little bit, but I'm not good with phone calls or talking all that much. Nova and Jacob chat every night, but Nova always makes a point to text me throughout the day, knowing I'll respond better to that. She's already finding ways to communicate with each of us and meet us where we're at.

Even with just communicating through text, we've learned a lot about each other. She somehow got me to talk about my parents, how they died, how I've dealt with it all. Nova, in turn, gave little pieces of herself and her past. I know she loves her mom, but I can tell her lack of attention to detail stresses Nova out, probably more than she even realizes. It has that protective instinct rearing up and wanting to take care of every little thing for her.

All of that only makes me miss her more. I crave her, ache for her in ways I can't even begin to understand. And I don't need to. All I need to know is that Nova will take my pain away. I should probably be afraid of how addicted to her I've already become, and part of me definitely still is. However, it helps to know Jacob is right there with me. I might be crazy, but he is too. If we go down, we go down together. And fuck, do I want to go down on Nova...

"Yo, Iz, stop daydreaming about Nova and come help me with this—"

There's a crash and then a loud, defeated groan coming from the kitchen. I dash over there to survey the damage.

I know I shouldn't, but I laugh when I see Jacob sitting on the floor with an empty pan next to him and a partially cooked turkey that's missing its legs rolling to a stop on the other side of the small kitchen. "Did you still need my help, or...?"

He flips me off, making me chuckle. It's a new feeling for me, this whole laughing business. Nova tumbled into my life and started opening up my heart from that very first day, making room inside of my chest for her light and happiness. It's made me lighter and happier as a result.

"I'm fine by the way, thanks for asking," he grumbles, making me smirk. I help Jacob up and grab some old rags and a bucket to help mop up the mess. Jacob curses and sputters under his breath as he wrestles the turkey onto the pan and then drops the whole thing into the sink.

"I guess I'll go change before figuring something else out for dinner," he mumbles, gesturing to his wet pants and shirt.

"Don't be too upset about it. She doesn't like us for our cooking skills. Or lack thereof," I tell him. Jacob grins, never one to be kept down for too long.

"That's the spirit," he winks.

As soon as Jacob steps into the bathroom to clean up, Nova knocks on the door. Are my palms sweaty? What is this, a junior high dance? No one has ever had this effect on me. I take slow, measured steps towards the front door, willing my heart to calm the fuck down.

What if I've built all of this up in my head? Jacob can be quite convincing when he wants to be, and we've been getting each other all worked up about claiming Nova. But we've only known her for less than a few weeks. It's crazy, right? This whole thing is crazy.

And then I open the door and stare into the golden eyes of my princess.

It's not crazy. None of it. It's so fucking real I'm having trouble breathing. Nova is more beautiful than I remember. Her auburn hair hangs loosely around her shoulders, framing her cherubic face with the cute button nose and full, lush lips. She's got on these skin-tight jeans that highlight her luscious body and have my cock raging hard in an instant. Fucking hell, I want to ride those curves until she screams for us and passes out from pleasure.

"Am I early?" Nova says, breaking through my lustful thoughts.

"You're perfect," I murmur before catching myself and shaking my head slightly. "I mean, you're right on time."

Nova smiles and lifts herself up on her toes, placing a sweet kiss on my jaw. I chuckle at how short she is, and then wrap my arm around her waist, hauling her into me and kissing my woman with all of the built-up lust and longing I have for her. Nova throws her arms around my neck and rubs her body against mine, matching the heated strokes of my tongue with a passion all her own.

When we finally part for air, I keep her close to me, resting my forehead on hers. I savor the way her shallow breaths feel across my skin, the rise and fall of her chest against mine, her coffee and cinnamon scent.

"I thought I made it all up," she whispers, burying her face into the side of my neck. I stroke her hair and hold her close to me.

"Made what up?"

She sighs and tilts her head up. "You. And Jacob. And what we did. And...and..." She darts her eyes away and bites her bottom lip. Jesus, she has no idea, no fucking clue how effortlessly sexy she is.

"And what, sweet girl? What else did you think you made up?"

"All the things...I mean the stuff...ugh!" She dips her head down and rests it on my chest. I kiss the top of her head and smile to myself. Looks like Nova is about as good at talking about her emotions as I am.

"We're very much real. And we're very much into you if that's what you're worried about." I feel her relax into my embrace, so I squeeze her tighter, not wanting to let her go. Unfortunately, Jacob has other plans.

"Kitten!" he exclaims from somewhere in the small cabin. I hear his big feet stomp ungracefully towards us.

I close the front door and turn to see Jacob with a fresh pair of jeans and a t-shirt partially on. When his eyes land on Nova, he tosses the shirt aside and strides towards her picking her up and crushing her into his bare chest, kissing the fuck out of her soft, pink lips.

Nova wraps her legs around Jacob's hips and clings to his shoulders as he turns around and walks to the kitchen. She breaks apart from his kiss and looks at me over Jacob's shoulder, her honey-colored eyes practically glowing with desire. When she licks her lips, my dick twitches and dribbles precum.

Jacob finally sets Nova down on top of the kitchen table, still standing in between her legs. I join them, reaching out to tuck some of Nova's silky hair behind her ear. She smiles at me and then at Jacob, running her hands up and down his torso. I bite back a groan at the thought of her doing that to me, too. All in good time. I don't want to overwhelm her, but goddamn, do I want her hands all over me.

"I've got good news and bad news, beautiful," he says, tracing her lips with the pad of his thumb.

"Hmm?" she responds distractedly, tracing the dips and grooves of Jacob's abs with her eyes and then her fingers.

Jacob chuckles and gathers up her hands, kissing one and then the other.

"About dinner..."

Nova finally looks behind Jacob and sees the disaster of a kitchen we hadn't cleaned up quite yet.

"Oh my God! Are you guys okay? What happened? Is that...is that a *turkey*?!" Nova bursts out laughing, making Jacob blush bright red. Watching my twin get all embarrassed after actually trying to impress a girl for the first time ever has got to be a highlight of my life. That and meeting Nova. And kissing Nova. And anything to do with Nova, really.

"Yeah, uh, I was cooking us dinner and then I sort of...dropped it..." Jacob shrugs. Nova grabs his face and kisses him sweetly.

"That is so nice of you, really it is, but that has to be a fifteen-pound turkey. Was that all for the three of us? I'm amazed it fit in that small oven!"

"I removed the legs and put them in a different pan and then squashed the bird down as far as I could before shoving it in."

Nova giggles, but then claps her hand over her mouth. Jacob is such a good sport. He doesn't care that he looks foolish right now, he's just happy that she's happy. I am, too.

"For someone who never cooks, starting with a turkey is awfully ambitious," Nova says, absent-mindedly drawing circles on Jacob's chest. I hardly notice her hand reaching out for me until our fingers are intertwined. I love that she wants to touch me, too, like we're all only complete when we're together.

"Yeah, you're probably right," Jacob admits. "When I think of our best memories growing up and here at the ranch, it's always around the dinner table with a big feast spread out, like at Thanksgiving. So I thought I'd give it a shot."

Nova's smile drops as she looks up at Jacob with unshed tears in her eyes. Her lower lip trembles as she gasps softly. "You made me a Thanksgiving dinner?" she whispers. The pain in her voice fucking guts me. I know Jacob is feeling the same way.

"Not exactly. I dropped an undercooked turkey on the floor, opened a can of cranberry sauce and a can of green beans, and I have a box of instant mashed potatoes I was going to whip up when the time came. It's not really much of a feast, per se—"

Nova throws her arms around Jacob's torso and hugs him tightly. Damn, now I wish I was the one who fucked up dinner. He rubs her back while I stroke her hair. Both of us exchange a look, unsure what's going on in our Nova's head right now but wanting to fix it all the same.

She takes a deep breath and leans back taking both of our hands in hers. "That's so thoughtful of you. It took a lot of planning. I've never had a real Thanksgiving dinner since it was just my mom and me, and the only thing she can make is cookies. So just...thank you."

"Anything for you, kitten. I'm just sorry it didn't work out. If we hurry, we can probably snag some leftovers from the main house," Jacob says.

"Oh. Uh...like, with everyone else? Jade, Noah, Teagan, and Knox?"

I smile as she finishes listing off everyone. The way she says their names you'd think they are celebrities.

"Is that a problem?" I ask, curious as to her tone.

"Yes. No, I mean no. But you said they are like your family."

"And...?" Jacob asks.

"And so, don't you think that's kind of crazy taking me to meet your family on the second date?"

Jacob shrugs. "We met yours."

Nova narrows her eyes at him, a sexy smirk tugging at the corner of her lips. "Yeah, but I didn't invite you over for dinner. I probably would have kept you and my mom apart as long as possible if given the choice."

I chuckle while Jacob feigns a sad puppy look. Nova laughs at him, making me chuckle even more. Her sassy little mouth, the way the sun streams in through the window and filters through her hair, the gleam in her eyes...it's all too much for me.

I reach out and cup her face, turning her head towards me and crashing my lips down on hers. My hand drifts down her neck and over her chest until I'm squeezing her plump breast and groaning into her mouth.

"What was that for?" Nova asks breathlessly when I finally manage to pull myself away from her.

"It had been entirely too long since the last time I did it, so..." I shrug, giving her a little grin. My chest tightens and my dick flexes when she grins right back at me.

Nova nods and grabs the front of my shirt, pulling me into her again. I groan and shove Jacob aside so I can step between Nova's legs. He protests for half a second, and then I hear him swear under his breath. I look over at him and see Nova grabbing his cock through his jeans, rubbing her little hand up and down his shaft while he gathers her hair away from her neck and kisses her there.

She looks up at me, her eyes pleading with me as she slips her hand underneath my t-shirt. "I want to see you, too," she whispers.

"Shit, princess, you can have whatever you want," I tell her before yanking my shirt off and pressing my body closer to hers. Nova moans, her eyes trailing up and down my chest, followed by her tiny, soft little hand. She traces my tattoos, her light touch scorching my skin and sending a shiver of anticipation down my spine.

Jacob bites down on her neck, making Nova cry out and claw my chest. I hiss out a breath and take her lips again, needing her taste on my tongue. Fuck, I need all of her sweetness on my tongue. I want her honey so damn bad. Fucking Christ, I feel like a wild animal, grinding into her, fisting her hair tightly as I hold her in place so I can devour everything she gives me.

My hands slide under her ass and I lift Nova up into my arms, walking her to my bed. She squeals and turns her head to look at Jacob. I can't see him, but I know he's on board for our new dinner plans.

Chapter 8

My head is still spinning from the last few minutes, but I don't mind. I feel safe right here in Isaiah's arms. How I went from feeling nervous to cherished to vulnerable to so incredibly turned on my pussy is gushing, I can't even explain, but I don't want to. It's them, Jacob and Isaiah. My twins. My men.

Isaiah sets me down in front of the large bed so gently, like he thinks I might break. Nothing could be further from the truth. I feel invincible when I'm with him and Jacob. I feel like I can let go for the first time in so long, maybe my whole life.

Jacob steps up behind me, running his fingers through my hair as he sweeps it to the side and nibbles on that sensitive spot right below my ear. I lean into him and tilt my head to the side, giving him better access. Isaiah trails a finger over my lips, down my chin, my throat, my breasts. He pauses briefly to circle one hardened nipple and then the other, before continuing on down my torso.

His hands play with the hem of my shirt and slip inside, roaming over my belly, squeezing the soft flesh. I instinctively suck my gut in, even more aware of my extra weight and every single one of my flaws now that I've seen how ridiculously sculpted Isaiah and Jacob are. They both have smooth, tanned skin, broad shoulders, thick arms, washboard abs, and those lines at their hips that point down in a V towards what I assume are massive dicks. How could they not be?

"Princess, what did I tell you?" Isaiah whispers into the shell of my ear, bringing me back into the present. He's still exploring my body with his rough, calloused hands, gliding them over my stomach, my wide hips, and the area I'm most self-conscious about – the rolls on my back.

I stiffen in his arms, but Isaiah growls, squeezing my back and pressing me deeper into his body like he wants to consume me completely.

"Your body is incredible," Isaiah murmurs, kissing down my neck.

"Fucking perfect," Jacob agrees, kissing down the other side of my neck while he palms my ass.

"Love these curves, Nova. I've been dreaming about them, rubbing my dick raw to thoughts of finally getting my hands on them," Isaiah continues.

A moan slips out of my mouth and my pussy clenches up tightly at his words. So dirty, yet so full of desire that I can't help but believe him.

"So goddamn sexy, kitten. I've been hard for you since I first laid eyes on you. It doesn't matter how many cold showers I take or how many times I take my cock into my fist and imagine sinking into your tight little cunt. I know it'll never measure up to the real thing. Never doubt how much we love your gorgeous body," Jacob says, rubbing his erection against me to prove his point.

Isaiah lifts my shirt up slowly, giving me plenty of time to protest. I have no intention of stopping him. If they want all of me, that's what they'll get. I want to be closer, to have their skin on my skin, their fingers inside of me again. I want to give them everything, feel them everywhere.

Lifting my arms, Jacob and Isaiah take my shirt off together and groan in unison as they uncover me. Isaiah immediately cups my breasts, covered in a black lacy bra, and pushes them together before licking up the center.

"Ohhh..." I gasp softly. Isaiah growls and buries his face deeper into my chest, pulling the cups of my bra down and devouring every inch of me with his teeth and tongue.

Jacob's big hands stroke up and down my sides and then reach forward, flirting with the waistband of my jeans. His fingers dip down and tease me, then he's fumbling with the button and zipper.

"Do you want me to stop, kitten?" he asks, his voice low and filled with so much need he sounds like he's in pain.

"Never stop," I moan, right as Isaiah bites down on my nipple.

One minute they are all over me, and the next minute they are backing away. I snap my eyes open in confusion, only to see Isaiah sliding my pants and panties down while Jacob unhooks my bra and slides the straps down my arms, kissing and nipping at my bare shoulders.

"Fuck," Isaiah growls, standing up and looking me over.

Jacob spins me around and sucks in air as his eyes roam up and down my curves.

"Nova...Jesus." He shakes his head, his eyes darting from my tits to my thighs, slowly making their way up to my dripping pussy, pausing there before he takes in the rest of me. "Beautiful. Goddess. Fuck me, Nova, you're absolutely stunning."

I know I'm blushing from head to toe with all of their attention and praise. It's more than I ever could have hoped or imagined for myself. How did I get so lucky to have not one, but two men worship and adore me? Part of me is scared this is too good to be true, but the bigger part of me, the part that has only recently awoken since meeting the twins, is saying fuck it, give them control and let them do whatever they want.

"Please..." I whimper, the needy word rising up and falling out of my mouth before I even know I'm saying it.

"Please, what, princess?" Isaiah grunts from behind me, his breath tickling the back of my neck.

"Touch me," I pant, the throbbing between my legs growing so intense it's almost painful. Isaiah's lips and nose trace a line back and forth across my bare shoulder and up my neck. "More," I whisper, looking right at Jacob.

He smiles wickedly and then crashes his lips down on mine, owning me completely. We finally break apart, gasping for air. Jacob kisses my throat, my collarbone, in between my breasts, and then kneels down in front of me, groaning when he sees how wet I am.

"Jesus," he growls, licking up the juices dripping down the inside of my thighs. My legs tremble, but Isaiah holds me steady, nuzzling my neck and massaging my breasts. I reach up behind me and tangle my fingers in Isaiah's hair, stretching myself out for my men to explore and touch me however they want. "Gonna eat this sweet little pussy now, Nova. I want you to cum on my tongue, kitten. Can you do that for me?"

I look down and see Jacob's green eyes turn almost black as he stares up at me with a feral look. I nod and lick my lips, a rush of liquid heat pouring out of me at the sight. Isaiah groans and trails one hand down my stomach and over my mound, dipping two fingers inside of my wet slit.

"You need to cum, don't you, princess? Need your men to take care of you?"

"Yes," I whisper, his words hitting me deep. I want that. I've always wanted that.

"We'll always take care of you, sweet girl," he whispers so only I can hear. "You're ours now."

With that, he circles my clit while Jacob guides one of my legs over his shoulder. Isaiah spreads two fingers on either side of my clit right as Jacob leans forward and licks up my center.

It's obscene, the way he's opening me up for his brother to eat me out. I look up at Isaiah and he kisses me deeply. I have two tongues inside of me, both fucking me and winding me up higher and higher. It's raw and unreal, what's happening between us.

I hiss in pleasure as Jacob devours my pussy and Isaiah plucks my nipples. I push myself into Jacob's face, desperate for relief from the ache he and his twin have caused inside of me.

Isaiah wraps a hand around my neck while squeezing my breast roughly with the other, causing my muscles to tense up deliciously. I can feel the power and strength surge through Isaiah's muscles as his fingers flex against my tender flesh. He's so in control, so dominant. And I love it.

Jacob growls into my pussy, sending vibrations radiating throughout my body as he laps at me in sloppy, ferocious strokes. I feel one finger slide inside of me, and then two, stretching me wide open and making me moan.

"So fucking tight, Nova, goddamn," Jacob grunts, curling up his fingers and tapping some spot inside of me that makes my entire body jerk and spasm. "There it is, fuck yes, again," he demands.

He hits that spot over and over, making me cry out and tremble while he and his brother hold me up. Isaiah removes his hand from my throat so he can grip my jaw and yank my face towards his for a punishing kiss. His hands slide down my body and grip my hips, hard, twisting them so Jacob has the perfect angle to sink his tongue deeper inside of me.

"I'm...oh God, I'm gonna cum," I tell them, my voice hoarse from all of my moaning, laced with a painful need.

"Cum hard, princess," Isaiah demands, grinding his jean-covered cock into my ass and biting the side of my neck.

Right before pure ecstasy hits, Isaiah slides his finger in my ass, pumping in and out while Jacob pries me open and sucks my clit. Hard. I pushed back into Isaiah's hand and then bucked my hips, taking even more.

I whisper for Isaiah to hold me tight, afraid I might fall from the intensity of what I'm feeling. I suck in a huge breath of air and let go completely. My body shakes and pulses, the orgasm coursing through my veins in violent jolts of pure bliss.

"Cum harder, Nova. Cum so fucking hard," Isaiah rasps, fucking my ass with his finger while Jacob drinks down my release.

I pull Jacob's hair and claw at his scalp as I'm hit with another explosion of overwhelming pleasure. I don't know how long I'm floating amongst the stars, but when I finally come back down, Jacob is cleaning me up with his tongue, making sure he gets every last drop. Isaiah has his strong arms around my waist, gently but firmly holding me against his chest.

"You did so good, princess," he praises, his voice low and comforting.

Jacob licks my clit, making me twist away from him. He pulls back and licks his lips. God, why is that so hot? "Sorry, kitten. I know you're sensitive. I just can't get enough of you."

I nod, my eyes never leaving his as he stands up and kisses me so tenderly, so reverently, I almost feel like crying. When we break apart, Jacob rests his forehead on mine, cradling my face in his hands and stroking my cheeks with his thumbs.

"That was amazing," I murmur, feeling the heat rise into my cheeks at my admission. Amazing doesn't even begin to describe what he just did to me, but it's a start.

"Fuck yeah, it was," he smiles, kissing me again, not so sweetly this time.

"Hottest goddamn thing I've ever seen," Isaiah says, placing a soft kiss on the side of my neck.

When I finally catch my breath, I'm aware of Jacob's thick shaft digging into my stomach, while Isaiah's digs into my backside. I'm overcome with a new wave of lust, needing to see my men naked.

I sink down to my knees between them and look up through my eyelashes, pleased to see two sets of deep green eyes go wide with shock. I stare at the freaking lead pipe in Jacob's pants and then look over at the equally as massive lead pipe in Isaiah's pants. I can't help but lick my lips.

"Fuck," Isaiah growls. Jacob groans at the same time, palming his cock and hissing.

"You don't have to do this," Jacob says, though I can tell it pains him to do so.

"What if I want to?" I ask. "You got to see me, I want to see you, too." I look up at Isaiah and chew nervously at my bottom lip before saying what's on my mind. "You said I was yours. Does that mean you're mine?"

"Yes," they both say at the same time.

I smile as butterflies erupt in my stomach. A warmth floods through me and fills me up. "Then let me see what's mine."

I giggle as both men scramble to get their pants and boxer briefs off, and then gasp as two enormous cocks spring out, almost hitting me in the face. My mouth waters and my hands move on their own, needing to touch the smooth, hard, angry-looking dicks in front of me.

Wrapping one hand around each of their massive shafts, I marvel at how hot they are. Jacob grunts, his cock twitching in my hand. I instinctively squeeze it harder, making him grunt again and thrust his hips into my hand.

Looking over at Isaiah, I see a drop of precum forming at the tip and then dripping down the bottom of his dick. Without thinking, I lean forward and lick it up, savoring the salty liquid on my tongue.

"Fucking hell, princess, that mouth…" I smile and open up, sliding his cock in between my lips and sucking him down as far as I can take him. Isaiah fists my hair, pulling it tight, and holding me down on his dick. "Shit, you feel so good," he groans.

Jacob's cock twitches again in my hand, so I begin pumping up and down as Isaiah guides my head along his shaft. I massage the throbbing vein on the underside of his length, causing him to thrust into my mouth, the tip of his cock entering my throat.

"That's it, kitten, suck his cock, take him deep. You look so fucking sexy like that," Jacob encourages me.

I suck harder, taking him deeper, swallowing him down and gagging on his thickness. Isaiah yanks me off of him and shoves my face towards Jacob's angry cock. I give him a questioning look, wondering if I did something wrong.

"Need a break, princess. You're too damn good at that. Show Jacob what that pretty little mouth of yours can do," Isaiah says.

I nod and lick my lips, turning my attention to Jacob. I kiss the tip of his dick, giggling when it swells up even more.

"Don't tease me, beautiful. I'm gonna cum all over your face if you're not careful."

"You say that like it's a punishment," I practically purr. Who am I right now? I don't know, but I don't care. I like this confident, sexy woman they bring out in me.

"Jesus Christ, woman, get your mouth on me right the fuck now," he growls.

I smirk at him, licking the drop of precum from the head of his cock and wiggling my tongue inside of the slit on top. Jacob groans painfully, the muscles in his stomach rippling as he tenses up.

Taking mercy on him, I open up and take him all the way into the back of my throat, gagging and swallowing him down, sucking so hard he starts trembling.

"Holy fuck, goddamnit, fuck, fuck, fuck," he roars.

I pull back and take him down, again and again, grabbing Isaiah's dick and fisting it as well, keeping him nice and hard for me. Then I switch, taking Isaiah into my mouth while pumping Jacob with my hand.

Both men grunt and groan for me, praising me and crying out their pleasure. I feel so powerful, so sexy, so incredibly fulfilled by what we're sharing. They took over my pleasure and now I'm taking over theirs.

"I'm gonna cum, kitten, fuck, I'm gonna cum so hard," Jacob grits out, the effort of holding off written all over his face.

"Me too, princess, Jesus, you're incredible."

I don't know what comes over me, but suddenly I know exactly how I want them to find their release.

"Cum on my tits," I beg, leaning back but still jerking them off in my hands.

"Fucking hell," Isaiah groans, thrusting his hips rapidly into my hand.

"Goddamn, kitten, so dirty for us," Jacob says, his voice tight with restraint.

Isaiah is the first to give up the fight, roaring out his climax as hot cum splashes over my chest and neck. Jacob cums a second later, hitting me with rope after rope of sticky cum on my tits. I keep stroking their throbbing cocks as more cum spurts out, landing on my chin and dripping down all over me. It's filthy and messy and so, *so* hot.

The next thing I know, Isaiah is lifting me up by my arms and tossing me onto the bed. Both men crawl up beside me and begin rubbing their cum into my skin, marking me as theirs. It's such a primal thing, claiming me like this, but I love it. I want it. I need it.

Jacob cups my face and turns me towards him, kissing me with everything he has. Isaiah does the same, my men leaving me breathless once again. I can still feel their hard cocks digging into my side. Aren't they supposed to go soft after an orgasm?

"I told you I'm always this fucking hard for you, beautiful," Jacob says, answering my unspoken question.

Isaiah growls and rolls on top of me, nudging my thighs open and laying his dick across my slit. He thrusts up and down, gliding his hard shaft through my soaking folds and tapping my clit.

This is it. He's going to take my virginity. Am I ready for that? I went from barely kissing anyone to falling into bed with *two* men, and it's all catching up to me right now. Isaiah senses the shift in my mood and stills, resting his forehead on mine.

"You okay, princess?" He asks.

I nod, but I'm not sure I mean it.

Isaiah kisses my temple and rolls off of me, tucking me into his side. Jacob snuggles up behind me and kisses my shoulder before resting his forehead there.

"S-sorry," I murmur, hating that I ruined the mood.

"Nova, there's nothing to apologize for," Isaiah assures me, his tone deep and calming. "We'll go at your pace, always. You're safe with us."

"Tonight was perfect, kitten," Jacob whispers into my ear before nuzzling into my neck. "Are you okay?"

I look at him over my shoulder and kiss him softly, smiling when he deepens it.

"I'm good," I tell him before looking over at Isaiah and letting him see the truth in my eyes. "I'm a little overwhelmed, but I feel so good. I know I'm safe with you. Both of you."

"Good, that's good, princess," Isaiah whispers, tucking my hair behind my ear and stroking my cheek. We lie there for a while, just holding each other and basking in the afterglow of our pleasure.

Eventually, I have to get up and get back home. Isaiah and Jacob take turns cleaning me up and helping me dress. It's just about the most adorable thing in the world the way they take care of me and want to make sure everything is perfect. With them in my life, I think everything just might be.

Chapter 9

Jacob

It's been three days since I've seen Nova, but I still taste her on my lips. She's exquisite. Sweet and tangy and all ours. Now that I've licked that decadent pussy, there's no way I can go without.

Our schedules have been crazy the last few days, but I'm determined to see her today. I miss her more than I thought possible, which I know is crazy considering how little we've actually seen her over the last few weeks but ask me if I give a fuck.

"Yo, Iz, what are you doing in there? Putting on makeup or some shit?" I call out impatiently.

Knox and Noah are back to working on the ranch, which means Isaiah and I finally have some downtime. I want to spend every moment with my kitten. Preferably in between her thick, juicy thighs, pounding her pink pussy into the mattress, but I'll give her all the time she needs to be comfortable with that.

I was so ready to go after our girl sucked us off and then demanded we cum on her tits. Jesus fucking Christ, that was hands down the sexiest thing I've ever seen. I will remember the unbridled lust in her eyes as we coated her chest with our seed for the rest of my life. Nova is a goddess. A queen. A sexy little minx who is just discovering the power she holds over us. Nova is all-consuming; the way she smells, the way she tastes, the way she cums with her whole fucking body, feeling every single thing until her pleasure is wrung from her very bones.

However, our Nova wasn't ready to take things to the next level, and I can respect that. We'll only ever do what she wants to give her the most pleasure. As much as I wanted to sink inside of her tight little cunt, I loved holding her in my arms, soothing her, playing with her hair as she drifted in and out of sleep. The times she was awake, we all talked in hushed tones, not wanting to burst the bubble of our peace and calm.

Nova told us about her mom, how she moved back here to take care of her. I assumed Miranda wasn't in the best of health since she rests a lot and needs Nova to be there for her more often than not. I never would have guessed she had cancer and was recovering from surgery.

Even though Nova told us Miranda's chance at beating it is high, I can see how it weighs on her. I can't imagine working such a physically demanding job and then taking care of a sick parent. Our girl is strong, resilient, and loyal. It makes me love her all the more.

I can't say exactly when it happened, but I'm ridiculously, unconditionally, obsessively in love with Nova. Maybe it was the first time she gave me a sassy remark. Or maybe it was when I bandaged her up and saw a sliver of her vulnerability. All I know is that somewhere between Nova stumbling out of her truck and feeling her lips wrapped around my cock, I fell in love.

"Seriously, Isaiah, I'm leaving for Roy's in two minutes with or without you!" I yell, hoping to hurry him up.

The bathroom door swings open and Isaiah glares at me. He's always been a slow mover, taking his sweet time getting out the door. Usually, I don't mind, but right now I'm about to jump out of my skin with the need to see Nova face to face. To be around her. Breathe in her cinnamon and coffee scent.

Twenty minutes later, we're pulling into Roy's Tavern to surprise Nova at work. It's mid-afternoon and I'm hoping the place won't be too busy yet with the dinner rush. I open the door and immediately scan the area for Nova. I see a flash of her auburn hair and turn to get a better view. She's wrapping silverware in the corner, looking tired and stressed. For a brief moment, I'm questioning our surprise visit. The last thing I want to do is overwhelm her.

But then Nova pops her head up and looks around her like she can sense our presence. When our eyes lock, her entire face lights up with the most beautiful smile in the world. My chest tightens up almost painfully at her pure, unfiltered joy. It's even sweeter knowing that Isaiah and I are the ones who put that look on her face.

I'm vaguely aware of someone standing in front of us asking about a booth or a table, but I ignore the woman, focusing instead on my kitten. She abandons her napkins and silverware and hops up, banging her knee on the table in the process. Both Isaiah and I wince, hating to see her hurt. Our girl is accident-prone, that's for sure.

Nova doesn't seem to notice her injury as she practically skips up to us.

"Hi," she says with so much happiness I'd swear she's in love. One can only hope because I'm right there with her. Isaiah might need a little more time to fully let her in, but I know he'll come around, too.

"Hey beautiful," I smile at her, kissing her cheek. She beams up at me and then looks over at Isaiah. He gives her a smile, something he's been doing a lot more of lately, and kisses her on her other cheek. The original waitress who was trying to seat us raises her eyebrows in speculation.

I probably should have thought this out a little more. I mean, we took her on our first date here, but things were pretty calm. This is something else entirely, showing up while she's on the clock, both of us giving her our attention and affection. Is it too much too soon? I know our relationship is unconventional, but I'm not ashamed of who we are and how we love. However, it's a big step, one that I didn't think through all the way. I've just been so desperate to see her, all the details sort of fell by the wayside.

Nova gives Isaiah the same bright smile she gave me, so I think we're in the clear. She grabs two menus and walks us to the booth she was sitting at before. She starts clearing off the silverware, but Isaiah stops her.

"Let us help," he insists, putting the tub of unwrapped silverware in the middle of the table along with the stack of napkins.

Nova narrows her eyes for a split second before breaking out into a grin. "What am I going to do with you two? Always wanting to help me and all. A girl could get used to that kind of treatment," she says with a wink.

"Good," I say, earning me an eye roll. God, I love her playfulness. "We'll always want to help you, kitten."

"And I can think of a few things you can do with us," Isaiah adds, his voice low so only we can hear.

Nova turns bright red, trying and failing to look indignant. She bites her lower lip and clenches her thighs together slightly, and fuck if my cock isn't growing harder by the second. Our girl wants us. Bad. Which is exactly where we want her.

"Can I get you guys anything?" she asks, ignoring Isaiah's comment as best she can. I open my mouth to tell her exactly what kind of meal I want, but she narrows her eyes at me and crosses her arms over her chest, pushing those mouthwatering tits up. "And *don't* say what you want to eat isn't on the menu."

Isaiah barks out a laugh, surprising all of us, while I chuckle and shake my head.

"Damn, am I that predictable?" I ask, grabbing up some silverware and wrapping a napkin around the bundle in the same way Nova is. Isaiah follows suit.

"You're that dirty-minded," Nova answers, her eyes shining with mischief.

"Don't forget my dirty mouth, beautiful. I don't remember any complaints about that."

Nova's eyes grow dark and her face flushes a pretty pink color. Goddamn do I want to bend her over this table and fuck that pussy raw and rough. The sound of Nova clearing her throat pulls me from my thoughts.

"Maybe I could hear some more of it later tonight?" she whispers, almost shyly, like she's not sure we'd agree. She's crazy, of course. It's all we've wanted since she left three days ago.

"Yes," Isaiah says huskily, clearing his throat. From the way he shifts in his seat I can tell he's trying to discreetly adjust himself. Fuck, I'm right there with him.

"Of course you can come over, kitten. What time do you get off work?"

"In an hour. I was here for breakfast and lunch, so I get to skip the dinner crowd, thank God. My feet are about to fall off," she sighs.

I hate that she's so tired all the time. Now that Knox and Noah are back at the ranch, I'll make a point to take time off and drive Miranda to her appointments and help out around the house. Nova shouldn't have to do it all on her own. After all, she's not alone anymore. She has us.

"Perfect. We'll meet you at our place for dinner?"

Nova gives me a skeptical look, one that makes Isaiah chuckle deeply. "Don't worry, I won't be doing the cooking. I think it's time you met the family."

"Really?"

"Hell yeah, beautiful. They've been dying to meet you."

"So they, um...know? About us?"

Isaiah nods while I smile. "Is that okay?" I ask.

"Y-yeah," she says, stuttering a bit. "I have to check on my mom and maybe...pack an overnight bag?"

Isaiah groans while I clench my fists under the table. "Fuck yes you can pack an overnight bag, Nova. We want you more than anything."

"There's no pressure though, princess," Isaiah says softly. "We just want to spend time with you."

Nova leans forward from where she's sitting across from us, getting as close as the table between us will allow.

"We can spend time together without our clothes though, right?" she whispers. Does she have any idea how close I am to bursting in my jeans? This woman owns me, body and soul, and right now my body is burning up with the desire to claim her once and for all.

"Fuck yes," Isaiah growls, earning us a few disapproving looks from the other patrons.

Nova smiles and bites her lip, then turns her attention to wrapping up the last of the silverware.

"Thanks for this," she sighs, reaching across the table to grasp our hands. Just that small touch makes my spine tingle. "For helping me with the silverware, for brightening my day. I've missed you guys," she confesses, darting her eyes away from us.

"We missed you, too," I promise. "So much." Nova smiles at me and then Isaiah, that confident sparkle back in her golden eyes. "Supper is at six, is that enough time for you?"

"That's perfect. Thanks again for coming to visit. I know you guys are busy."

"Not too busy for you," Isaiah says.

Nova is called away to help out at a few tables. She flits around the place, stopping by our table to drop off the pie we ordered. Isaiah and I eat in silence, which is normal for us.

We finished our pie a while ago, but neither one of us makes a move to get up and pay our bill. We just want to be around her.

Eventually, however, we do need to head back to the ranch. Isaiah leaves for the bathroom while I settle up our tab. Out of the corner of my eye, I see Nova at a table with a bunch of younger guys, probably around her age. One of them looks familiar, but I can't quite place him.

I don't like the weaselly look in his eyes, especially when he's looking at my kitten like that. I can't hear what he's saying, but her face scrunches up in anger. I see her square her shoulders and tell him off. Good girl.

She storms off towards the back of the restaurant and I follow closely on her heels.

"Hey, is everything okay? What did those asshats say? Do I need to punch their fucking teeth in?"

Nova laughs, which allows me to relax a bit. "Nothing I can't handle," she says, though her eyes give her away. She's bothered by whatever happened, but she clearly doesn't want to talk about it.

I give her a long look and then nod my head once. "I'll let it slide for now, but kitten, please tell me if those dicks bother you again, alright?"

She nods and gives me a genuine smile this time. I give her a kiss on the forehead, though all I want to do is press her against this wall and devour her lips. "See you later tonight, beautiful."

"I can't wait," she grins at me, that megawatt sparkle back in her eyes. I have to walk away before I jump the gun and tell her I love her.

***

Nova was nervous about meeting everyone, though she didn't need to be. Everyone loved her, just like I knew they would. What's not to love? Jade and Teagan even made plans to hang out with her later, which I know meant the world to Nova. She doesn't have many friends, especially since moving back here and working while taking care of her mom.

After saying our goodbyes, Isaiah and I led her back to our place. The air has been thick with so much built-up need and desire between the three of us, but Isaiah and I didn't want to maul Nova as soon as we walked in the door to our cabin.

Well, we very much *did* want to maul her, and still do, but we want her to be comfortable here and feel safe to explore with us and take her time. So, instead of bending her over the couch and fucking her senseless, we lit a fire in the fireplace and curled up on the couch.

Nova is on Isaiah's lap with her feet stretched out over my lap while I give her a foot rub. She sighs so sweetly and rests her head on Isaiah's shoulder.

"That feels amazing," she breathes out. I smile at her and dig my thumbs into the heel of her left foot. Nova moans, making my dick stand at attention.

Isaiah threads his fingers in the hair at the nape of her neck and tugs, angling her face so he can kiss her. She gasps and then clutches his shirt, pulling him closer. Our girl is trembling with just as much need as we have. I inch my fingers up her legs, massaging her ankles and calves before tickling the sensitive skin behind her knees.

Nova opens her legs, giving me a glimpse of the black lacy panties she's hiding under her dress. Good fucking God, I can't take it. My mouth waters at the thought of sucking the juices from her panties before spearing her tight little cunt with my tongue and getting it straight from the source. I remember her taste, her smell, the way her thighs felt against my face while I brought her higher and higher and then dropped her off the edge of oblivion.

Isaiah growls into her mouth and grips her hips, positioning her so she's straddling him.

"*Ooooh...*" Nova moans, instantly grinding down on him. Her fingers dig into his shoulders as she rocks back and forth, up and down, finding what works for her.

Jesus, it's so hot watching her and Isaiah like this. I feel like it's a little show just for me. I get to watch my sexy as fuck kitten find her pleasure with my brother - my twin brother - while building the anticipation for myself.

Before I realize what I'm doing, I have my dick out, stroking up and down my hard length while Nova moans and writhes on top of Isaiah. I grunt and squeeze the base, trying not to cum yet. I'll save that for Nova. She deserves all my cum, wherever she wants it.

Nova gasps for air, breaking the connection between her and Isaiah so she can look directly at me. When she sees what I'm doing, her pupils dilate even more, and she licks her lips before trailing her eyes up my body and finally resting them on mine.

"Like what you see, beautiful?" I ask, my voice low and scratchy from trying to hang on to some sort of control.

"Mmhm," she murmurs, looking down again at my fist where it's wrapped around my length and then back into my eyes.

I stare right at her as I jerk off, and she never breaks eye contact. Not even when Isaiah starts squeezing her ass and sucking on her neck. Nova just moans and rocks her hips, still staring right at me. It's so intense, so erotic, so fucking everything.

Suddenly, Nova pushes off of Isaiah's lap, standing up on shaky legs. I worry that it was too much for her, but she surprises the hell out of me by whipping her dress over her head and reaching out towards us, encouraging us to take her hands.

Isaiah does one better and throws her over his shoulder, bolting to his bed. Nova squeals and giggles, then lifts her head up and smiles at me with lust and excitement. Isaiah tosses her down on the bed and then falls on top of her, holding himself up with a hand on either side of her head.

I finish taking off the rest of my clothes, watching as they kiss passionately. Isaiah reaches behind her and unclasps her bra, setting those perfect tits of hers free. I growl and climb up next to her reaching out to massage one breast and then the other. Nova looks over at me with such desperate longing in her eyes, I can't help but ravish her soft, wet mouth.

Isaiah groans and moves down her body, kneeling on the floor between her legs and lifting them over his shoulders, making her shake and pant for air. I take the opportunity to kiss and nip down her neck while Isaiah does the same to her inner thighs.

"Jacob got to taste you and now I want my turn. Fair is fair," he grunts right before ripping off her panties.

"Hey!" she scolds, though it sounds more like a moan than a reprimand. "You both owe me a pair of panties."

Isaiah doesn't say anything, he just dives right in and sucks that sweet pussy while I kiss the air right out of her lungs.

"I'll buy you a closet full of panties," I tell her in between kisses. "Preferably lacey little thongs with ties on the side for easy access."

"Or you could just never wear panties again," Isaiah adds, slipping a finger inside of her tight little hole and groaning. My fingers itch to touch her there as well, to feel her wet heat squeeze around me like a vice.

Nova shivers at his words, making him chuckle darkly. Then he dips his head down and sucks on her clit while pumping his fingers in and out of her. She bows her back off the mattress, shoving those gorgeous tits in my face. I suck on one nipple and then the other, licking and nipping her sensitive flesh while Isaiah devours her cunt.

"Oh...ohmygod, it's, it's, I'm..."

"Do it, kitten, let go," I growl, tweaking one nipple while gently biting down on the other.

She claws at the sheets and tips her head back, opening her mouth in a silent scream. I hear Isaiah growl, the sound muffled by her pussy, and then Nova explodes, tensing and trembling in our arms. I look over her body, a blush spreading down her neck and chest, all the way to her belly button. Her tummy jiggles a little as she rides out her orgasm, the sight making my mouth water. I want to bite and lick every single inch of her, devour her whole, and then start all over.

Nova has her thighs locked around Isaiah's head as he continues to lap at her and drink down every drop. He shakes his head back and forth, making Nova cry out and slap the mattress as she fucking cums again. I cup her chin and tilt her head up so I can kiss her while she comes back down.

"Fuck," Isaiah growls, sitting back on his haunches and staring at Nova's pussy.

"Delicious, isn't she?" I ask, already knowing the answer.

"Best goddamn dessert in the whole fucking world."

I look back at Nova, who has an arm flung over her face, shielding her eyes as her chest rises and falls with labored breaths.

"You okay, kitten?" I murmur, placing a delicate kiss on her arm and then lifting it up so I can see her beauty.

She nods, finally opening her eyes. "So good," she whispers, biting her lip. Jesus, she's ready to go again. I can tell by the way she squirms and then reaches out for my neck, pulling me down for a heated kiss.

Isaiah joins us on the bed, completely naked, kissing up Nova's torso and nibbling on her breasts. I pull away from those addictive lips and reach down to stroke her pussy, keeping her right there, right on the edge for us, ready and willing and so fucking wet.

"Please," she whimpers, her eyes begging me to do something about her state of arousal.

"What do you want, beautiful? I need you to tell me."

"I..." she trails off, blushing bright red. I stop circling her clit, making her narrow her eyes at me. I smirk and wait for her to finish her sentence.

"Tell me," I demand. My tone lights a fire in her eyes, which has my cock twitching and leaking precum. She's going to be so damn dirty for us, I can already tell.

"Fuck me," she whispers. "P-please," she adds. So fucking cute.

I groan, dipping one finger into her entrance and then another, scissoring them deep inside of her to stretch her out for me. Isaiah lifts his head up from where he's been sucking on her tits and kisses her so tenderly.

"Are you sure, princess?" he whispers onto her lips.

"Yes, I want it. I need it. I'm so achy, please take it away, please..."

"Shit, Nova, we need you too, kitten. So goddamn sexy, so fucking hot for us, aren't you?" I grit out as I position myself in between her legs. Nova nods, spreading her thighs to accommodate me.

"Wider, beautiful," I whisper, kissing her temple and running my nose along the shell of her ear.

Isaiah grips one of her legs and pries her open for me. I hold myself up on one forearm next to the side of her head, and then grip my cock, sliding the head up and down her slit, gathering her juices and spreading them up and down my length.

Resting my forehead on hers, I breathe in her warm, earthy scent mixed with her arousal. "Please," she whispers, moving her hips to try to get me where she wants me. "I need more, I need you."

Hearing the desperate plea in her voice has the last thread of my control snapping. I slam into her, shocked when I break through her virginity. She cries out and tenses up, burying her head in my neck to muffle her sounds.

She's ours. All ours. Only ours. Christ, I can't believe it. A virgin. A fucking perfect goddess who will depend on us and only us for her pleasure from this day forward.

"Breathe for me, Nova. I didn't know, beautiful, I didn't know it was your first time."

I hear Isaiah groan low in his chest, no doubt having the same possessive thoughts I'm having. I hate that I hurt her though. I'd like to say that I'd have gone slower if I knew, but honestly, I don't think I could have. I stay still inside her, nudging her head back so I can kiss away the tears sliding down her cheeks. Isaiah kisses her other cheek, both of us taking care of this need of hers too.

"I wanted it. I still want it," she says on a shaky breath. "It's perfect. Please don't stop."

"Never," I grunt, pulling out of her slowly and looking down at my cock. It's coated in her cream and tinged with the slightest bit of pink from taking her cherry. I growl at the sight, committing it to memory.

"Get back here!" she whines, making me snap my eyes up to hers.

I smirk at our feisty little Nova, never breaking eye contact as I slowly push my thick dick back inside of her cunt, marveling at the fact that I'm the first one in here.

"Greedy little thing, aren't you?"

"Apparently."

She barely gets her cheeky response out before she's moaning and bucking her hips, lodging me deeper inside of her. I hiss out in pleasure as her pussy throbs around me, her inner muscles squeezing me so fucking tight. It's unlike anything I've ever felt.

Nothing compares to being connected to Nova in the most intimate of ways. Sex has never been like this for me. Knowing Nova the way I do, loving her as much as I do, all the time we've taken to explore each other and have real conversations...it all makes this so much more meaningful, so much more vulnerable.

"You feel incredible, Nova. So fucking good. This pussy was made for us, wasn't it?"

"Yes, fuck me, break me, I'm yours."

Isaiah grunts, a deep, gravelly, pained sound. Out of the corner of my eye, I see him fisting his cock, jerking himself up and down in hard, almost violent strokes as he stares at where she and I are connected.

"I'll give you everything, beautiful. Everything you want," I vow before pulling out of her and then snapping my hips, piercing her with one hard thrust.

"Oh!" she screams, wrapping her legs around my hips while I tunnel in and out of her tight little pussy, building her up, breaking her in, fucking her roughly. Far too roughly for her first time.

I pause inside of her, catching my breath and searching her face for any sign of distress.

"Don't stop, are you kidding me?"

Isaiah chuckles at her outburst. I would too, except I'm about to explode and I need her to get there first.

"Just making sure you're okay," I say through clenched teeth.

Nova unwraps her legs from me and plants her feet on the bed, thrusting herself up and grinding on me. I groan and hold my breath, reveling in the way she's taking control, chasing her pleasure, using my dick to get herself off.

When I can't take anymore, I grip her hips, pinning her in place so I can pound into her.

"Yes, yes, yes, like that, oh God, oh…"

"Jesus, you gotta cum for me, Nova, I can't hold on…fuck, baby, cum for me."

I piston in and out of her, reaching down between us and wiggling my thumb over her clit. Isaiah cups her cheek and turns her face towards him so he can kiss her while I fuck into that tight little cunt for all I'm worth.

I feel her tense around me as she breaks away from Isaiah. He plays with her tits while she stares right at me, a wild, desperate look in her eyes. I'm right there with her. I'm completely feral, all animal in this moment as I rut into her.

Nova whimpers with each shallow breath, her body trembling underneath me. She's right there, I can tell. I twist my hips and slam my cock into her G-spot, making her cum instantly. Her orgasm is an infinite refrain of whimpers and moans. She unravels before my eyes, liquefying right into my hands. I growl and fuck her hard, so hard, and then my orgasm rushes out of me almost painfully as I burst inside of her.

"Fucking Christ, Nova," I mumble, burying my face into the side of her neck and pumping in and out of her slowly, prolonging our pleasure until I can't hold myself up anymore.

Rolling to the side, I kiss her forehead and stroke her back, feeling her shiver and struggle to catch her breath.

"You okay, kitten?"

"Mmhm," she sighs, resting her little hand on my cheek and kissing me sweetly.

I gently turn her to face Isaiah, who I can tell is about to lose his damn mind. "Have fun, beautiful," I whisper into the side of her neck before pressing a kiss there.

She opens her mouth to say something, but Isaiah cuts her off with a kiss. I smirk and get off the bed to clean up. Fuck if my dick isn't already half hard. I hope Nova is up for rounds three and four and five. I'll never get enough.

Chapter 10

Fuck. Fuck, fuck, *fuck*.

A virgin. She was a virgin. I can't quite wrap my head around that. On a primal level, I'm possessive as fuck and vibrating with the need to beat my chest and roar out our claim on her. But there's a twinge of doubt. This is real. So fucking real.

I think I love her. Hell, I think I've loved her all along, but there's something about this, about finally being together like this, knowing Jacob and are the first to stretch her little pussy out... Goddamn. It makes me want to slow down and take a breath.

It also makes me want to split her open with my swollen fucking cock and break her cunt just like she asked us to.

Nova reaches out for me, combing her fingers through my hair almost reverently. Her touch is tender, but her eyes shine with a dark and desperate need. The combination is my undoing. I'll sort through my messy feelings later.

I turn Nova on her side so she's facing me. Trailing my fingers up her thighs, I follow the rounded curve of her hip and the slight dip of her waist, up, up, up, until I cup her cheek and draw her closer to me.

"Are you okay, sweet girl?" I murmur before kissing her forehead. My wild lust claws at me from the inside, but I think she needs this reassurance from me right now. I also need her to tell me she's ready for me. Jacob wasn't gentle and I don't think I can be either.

"I know I should probably be overwhelmed or at the very least worn out, but I'm not. I just want you. So bad. I want to feel you, too. I want that connection. I need it. Does that make me slutty?"

"What?" Her words are a punch to the gut. "Hell no. Other people might not understand what we have, but who the fuck cares? I'm not ashamed of you, of us, and I don't want you to be ashamed either. It's fucking hot that you want us both. It's perfect. You're perfect."

Her soft smile lets me know I said the right thing. Then her eyes gleam with mischief, and I know she's ready to play. Nova bites her bottom lip and grabs the back of my neck, pulling me closer, until our lips are millimeters apart.

"I can be slutty for you though, right?" she whispers before pulling my bottom lip between her teeth and biting down enough to sting. I growl into her mouth and mold our lips together, claiming her, fucking her with my tongue the same way I plan on doing with my huge cock. Mercilessly.

Nova pulls away from me, gasping for air. I take the opportunity to roll on my back, taking her with me so she's straddling me. Nova gasps and steadies herself on my chest, smiling at me wickedly.

The little minx starts rubbing her pussy against my cock, dripping her juices all over me and driving me insane.

"Princess..." I groan, grabbing her hips and sinking my fingers into the soft flesh. I want to lift her up and spear her with my dick, but I still her movements instead. "Are you sure you're ready? You're not too sore?"

"I promise I'm okay. Except that I want you to fuck me, and for some reason, you're stalling," she adds.

"Jesus," I grunt, helping her grind down on me once again.

"I wish I could give you my virginity too. I wish it could have been both of you somehow."

I pull her down onto my chest, trapping my dick between our bodies. Tangling my fingers in her hair, I tug on the strands until she's looking at me. "Don't you worry about that, sweet girl," I tell her, my voice rough and on edge. I keep one hand gripping her hair, and trail the other one down her back, squeezing her juicy round ass. "You saved something else for me, didn't you?" She hums and then presses back against my hand. I dip a finger into her slit, dragging up her cunt juice and circling her tight, puckered ass hole, applying slight pressure.

"Yessss..." Nova hisses.

I grunt in approval, pushing the tip of my finger inside. "I'm going to take this ass, princess. I'll ride you rough and dirty, fill you up, stretch you out so I can slide in there any time I want. And you'll love it. You'll beg me for it, my sweet, dirty girl."

Nova moans and kisses me with such fierceness I swear to Christ I could cum from that alone.

"I want it," she pants. "I want everything," she says in between her wild kisses. I slide my finger in deeper, then add a second finger, pumping in and out of her. She writhes on top of me, her body trembling with the need for release.

Fuck, her tight little ass hole pulses around my fingers. I can just imagine the way she's going to feel when it's my cock instead. Mustering up all the strength I have left, I withdraw my fingers.

"Not today, Nova. I need to stretch you out. I also need inside of that pussy before I lose my goddamn mind."

"Yes, please," she moans. Her eagerness is going to be the death of me. I don't think I'll ever be able to turn her down when she's offering herself up to me so freely, so full of desire. She's not trying to shy away from it, which is hot as fuck.

I release her hair from my grip and push her up, lifting her hips so she's hovering over me. Nova grins and nestles her soaking wet pussy right on the tip of my dick. She wiggles her hips a little bit to get herself lined up, pulling a strangled noise from the depths of my being. She's already too fucking good at this.

I almost lose my shit when she stares down at me, her nostrils flaring, her pupils blown wide, her big, round tits bouncing with every labored breath she takes.

"Go slow, Nov—"

"Fuck yes!" she cries out as she impales herself on my hard cock. "Ohmygod, so deep, so, so deep... I can't believe I'm gonna..." Her pussy contracts and creams all over me as Nova digs her nails into my chest, shouting out her climax.

"Goddamn motherfucking Christ!" I roar as my balls draw up tight and I explode inside of her. Fuck, fuck, fuck, I wanted this to last longer, too fucking good, so goddamn hot and tight.

I flip her over on her back and pound into her, filling her up with my cum until it leaks out of her. My dick is still rock hard, so I keep hammering into her, keep snapping my hips, keep fucking her through her orgasm as she whimpers and gasps for air.

Her sounds make my bones vibrate. I grunt as her nails dig into my shoulders and score my flesh, my cock hitting home in one hard thrust after another. The scorching hot sensation of her tight muscles around me makes me gasp into her mouth. Her lips fall open in a silent scream as she takes me in and stretches around me. I rest my sweaty forehead on hers, gritting my teeth against yet another orgasm threatening to overtake me.

"Isaiah, you feel so good, so, so, good, please..." she whimpers.

"Please, what, princess?"

"M-more...I need...I need...I'm close already..."

"I've got you, dirty girl," I growl, sitting back on my haunches so I can grab her wrists and pin them above her head. Nova squeezes her thighs around my waist as her liquid heat coats my cock, letting me know she likes it.

I glide my free hand up her luscious body and wrap my fingers lightly around her throat.

Her pussy clamps down on me almost painfully as she tenses and moans. I ghost my nose and lips up and down the shell of her ear, her shallow breaths and desperate whimpers a beautiful soundtrack I can't get enough of.

"Is this what you need, princess?" I growl, tightening my hand around her neck slightly. She nods and squirms beneath me as I slide my cock through her folds slowly, so slowly. "Are you a filthy fucking girl? You want me to choke your orgasm out of you?"

"Yes, it's so wrong, but I want...I need it," she pleads.

"Nothing we do is wrong, Nova. Not as long as we both want it. You're fucking perfect."

With that, I pull back and slam my cock into her over and over, the sloppy wet sounds filling the room, joining her cries of ecstasy.

"Oh fuck," Jacob says, entering the room. "Fucking hell, holy shit," he groans, climbing on the bed next to us, taking in the scene.

Nova darts her eyes over to Jacob, staring right at him, grunting and moaning as I tear into her savagely and grip her neck firmly.

"Christ, kitten," he growls, fisting his cock and grunting right along with her.

Our girl is an animal. She's insatiable, exquisite, dirty, and yet so fucking pure.

"Need to cum now, princess," I rasp, my body shuddering as my orgasm crawls down my spine, making it tingle deliciously. "Cum right the fuck now!" I roar, squeezing her neck and fucking that pussy as hard as I can.

Nova freezes, her muscles tight, her breathing non-existent as her eyes roll into the back of her head.

Then she shatters in my arms.

I let go of her neck and wrists, placing a fist next to her head and gripping her hip with my other hand. I hold her still while I piston in and out of her, making her tits jiggle obscenely with each rough thrust.

Nova reaches out and grabs Jacob's cock, jacking him off even as she's in the throes of her own climax. Jacob curses and slides his hand in between us, circling her clit. Nova keeps coming, keeps crying out, keeps convulsing.

I hold myself still inside of her and unleash a torrent of cum so forcefully I think I might pass out. At the same time, Jacob explodes on Nova's chest and then falls on his back, next to Nova while I collapse on her other side.

We're all struggling to even breathe in the aftermath of the most intense sexual experience we've ever had. Or, at least, it's the most intense experience I've ever had. Jesus. I've never cum so hard.

I manage to turn my head towards Nova, but even that movement felt like it took all of my energy. This woman fucked my goddamn brains out.

Nova's eyes are closed, her brow furrowed slightly. My heart stops in my chest at the thought of hurting her. I fucked her so, so hard. I choked her for Christ's sake, held her down while I rutted into her.

"Nova, look at me," I say, trying to keep my voice calm even though I'm panicking a bit inside. She opens her eyes and shivers, her breath hitching in her throat. I reach out and tuck some of her hair behind her ear and cup her face. "Are you okay, princess?"

Jacob rolls onto his side, spooning himself around Nova and kissing the top of her head.

"It hurts..." she whispers. Her words slice through me like a hot blade, twisting and tearing my heart out. "So good," she finishes. "A good ache. So good," she says again.

"I hurt you?"

"No. Well, yes, but I needed it. Wanted it." I let out a deep breath and allow my muscles to relax a bit. "You said nothing was wrong if we both wanted it, right? Or was that too much?"

"Fuck no, Nova. You were incredible. What we shared was...God, it was unlike anything in this whole goddamn world. But you're so young. So inexperienced."

She grins, lifting an eyebrow up and giving me a look that makes my cock twitch, even though the fucker is sore and raw and should be out of commission for a while. "I think I'm pretty experienced now, don't you?"

Jacob groans behind her and I can't help but take her puffy, swollen lips in a kiss. It's gentle this time, full of promises and the tenderness I should have shown her all along.

"Hey," she whispers when I release her lips from mine. "That was amazing. I loved what we did. It was special and perfect."

I rest my forehead on hers and close my eyes. How did she know what I was thinking? How can this woman know me so well already? "Perfect," I murmur. "Like you."

Nova laughs softly and then yawns dramatically, making Jacob and I laugh.

"Tired, beautiful?" Jacob asks, rolling her on her back and propping himself up on an elbow so he can look down at her.

She nods, her eyes drooping as she melts into the mattress. I lean over and kiss her temple before rolling off the bed. "Be right back," I say when she gives me a curious look. A few moments later, I return to my princess with a warm washcloth to clean her up. Jacob and I take turns running the cloth over her thighs, her pussy, her chest where Jacob came on her. We should probably get her in a bath, or at the very least, a shower, but our girl is already half asleep.

I toss the washcloth in the general direction of the dirty laundry basket and climb back into bed with Nova. Jacob settles himself on her other side and pulls the blankets over us. Nova sniffles, one tear falling down her round, creamy cheek.

"Nova? What is it?" Fuck, I did hurt her. I'll never forgive myself.

"I'm okay," she says, reassuring me. "You both just...you took care of me. All of me, even when I didn't know what I needed. I was scared to let go and give up control, but you both make it easy."

I don't know what to say to that, but it feels damn good to hear her say she wanted to give us control, that she trusted us that much.

"Always, kitten," Jacob murmurs, kissing her temple. "Whatever you need, whenever you need it."

She turns towards Jacob and kisses him sweetly on the mouth and then faces me and does the same. "Thank you," she whispers right before yawning again.

Jacob chuckles and rolls Nova closer to him so they are face to face. Wrapping an arm around her waist, I curl up behind her, holding her close. I feel her breaths deepen and even out, the weight of her body finally relaxing as she lets go of consciousness and drifts off to sleep.

I look over her head at Jacob, who is also sound asleep. I'm exhausted as well, but I stay up and watch Nova sleep. Creepy, I know, but I can't stop. She's everything. I can't fuck it up. I'm suddenly terrified of losing her. Of getting hurt. Of hurting her. I feel like I'm being ripped open, exposing my most vulnerable parts and praying she doesn't end me.

Nova stirs in her sleep and looks at me over her shoulder. "I'm not gonna hurt you, Isaiah. You mean too much to me," she says softly.

"How did you know what I was thinking?" I whisper close to her ear.

She smiles and turns towards me, placing her hand on my cheek. "I don't know everything about you yet, but I still know you. I feel you. I'll protect all of the little pieces of your heart you keep showing me."

Her words heal a wound deep inside of me I wasn't even aware of until she covered me with her goodness and light. I rub my nose back and forth against hers. "My sweet girl," I murmur, my voice thick with emotion.

"Why do you only call me that when it's just us?"

I pause briefly, deciding if I want to tell her the truth. Kissing the tip of her nose, I lean back so I can look at my Nova while giving her yet another piece of my heart.

"My ex cheated on me. It left some wounds, ones that I didn't think would ever heal. Until you. I know it's silly, but..." I take a deep breath and continue. "I like that we have something that's just for us, you know?"

I worry that I may have said too much or made her think I want to steal her away from Jacob, which couldn't be further from the truth.

Nova smiles and rests her forehead on mine. "I love that," she whispers. "I lo... I, um, I love that," she says all in a rush. I know what she's not saying, or rather, what she caught herself from saying. The thought of her falling as hard for me as I am for her settles something deep inside of me. I won't make her repeat herself or embarrass her. It's enough to know she feels it.

"I love it too," I say, letting the implication hang between us. Tucking her head under my chin, I breathe in her coffee and cinnamon scent and soak up the warmth radiating off of her soft skin.

Nova sighs contentedly and curls up, snuggling closer like she wants to disappear inside of me. I think I want that, too.

Chapter 11

Nova

I wake up to light streaming through a crack in the curtains over the window. It's just enough light to see my two men tangled up in me. Even though my muscles are sore and my pussy is worn out, I can't help but smile. It's a delicious kind of ache, one I hope to experience again and again.

My entire body heats up with the memory of last night. It was beyond anything I could have ever imagined for my first time, or *any* time, really. I didn't think I'd ever have the kind of mind-melting, soul-shattering sex you only find in smutty romance books. That life wasn't for me, and I never thought twice about it.

Ha. Twice. Taken by my twins, twice in one night. Holy hell, it was amazing. I have always been self-conscious of my curves, but Jacob and Isaiah showed me how much they love my body. It gave me the confidence to ask for what I wanted. I was a little surprised by the dark desires that rose to the surface, and then at the vulnerability that swept through me when we were done, but my men took care of me in every single way.

God, was I taken care of. I can't even remember how many times I came last night. More than I ever thought possible, that's for sure. And harder, too. My pussy clenches just thinking about how rough they were, how urgent their thrusts, how desperate their need.

Is it too soon to fall in love? Does that make me the cliché virgin? But no, they have to be feeling it. Jacob and Isaiah made me feel so cherished. So dirty, yes, but so precious.

For some reason, that asshole's remark from the diner yesterday filters through my thoughts.

"I didn't know you were into such kinky shit. When you're done fucking those two cowboys, come take us for a spin. Three is better than two, right? Be our little whore, Nova."

Fucking Tim. I don't understand where his sudden obsession with me came from. He made all four years of high school a living nightmare for me, always teasing me about my weight and trying to get me to break. Now he wants me to fuck him and his dipshit lackeys? No way.

I shake my head clear of those thoughts. I won't let him ruin this for me.

Looking over at Jacob, I smile as he sleeps peacefully, a shadow of a grin on his lips, like always. I turn my head and look at Isaiah, who is also asleep, but with a more serious face. They are both so beautiful in their different ways.

My heart hurts as I remember what Isaiah said before we went to sleep. I know there's more to the story than he told me, but I'm thankful he chose to share anything at all. He's definitely more reserved than Jacob, more guarded. Jaded. Bitter. I want to show him he's amazing and that his ex was a moron for cheating.

But first I have to check on Mom. I told her I was staying at a friend's house last night. She smiled and gave me a knowing look. My mom's free-spirited ways may have caused issues in the past, but I am thankful she's so non-judgmental about Jacob and Isaiah. Not only doesn't she judge, but she seems genuinely supportive and happy for us.

I slowly untangle myself from Jacob and Isaiah, not wanting to disturb their sleep. I'm almost completely free from their possessive hold on me, when an arm snakes around my hips, pulling me back into a warm, hard chest.

Isaiah grumbles something and then buries his face into my hair, kissing my head so sweetly. I smile at the rough, tattooed, cowboy being all snuggly in the morning. Turning in his arms, I kiss the tip of his nose, my heart tripping all over itself when I see Isaiah's beautiful, long lashes flutter against his cheeks.

When he finally opens them, he stares right at me and smiles so warmly I'm finding it hard to breathe. He's so pure and impossibly sweet in this moment. Yeah, I'm definitely in deep with these two. Totally head over heels.

"I have to grab my phone and check on mom," I explain, keeping my voice low so as not to wake Jacob. I give Isaiah a quick kiss on the lips and then pull away from him, only to feel his hand wrap around the back of my neck, pulling me in for a scorching hot kiss.

We finally break apart, my lungs on fire from lack of oxygen. "Just wanted you to remember what you're leaving behind," he says, his voice rough and deep.

I giggle and roll my eyes at him, loving his over-the-top possessiveness even though I'm only going a few feet away to grab my phone.

Pushing myself away from him, I almost make it to the edge of the bed before I'm being pulled back again, by Jacob this time. He presses sweet kisses on my forehead, eyelids, cheeks, nose, and finally my lips. He deepens our kiss, letting his hands wander down my back until he grips my ass and squeezes. Hard.

I pull away from him, but he follows me, taking my lips again until I'm out of breath for the second time this morning.

"You...two..." I pant, flopping down on my back between them. "I'm just going to grab my phone, no need to maul me," I tease.

"Mmm, that's where you're wrong, princess," Isaiah says, his voice dark and rumbling up from his chest.

"There's always a need to have your sweet, sexy lips against mine," Jacob adds, rubbing his thumb back and forth over my lips.

I nip at his thumb playfully, making him groan. I use the opportunity to hop up and crawl off the bed. I look over my shoulder and see both men pouting. It's too freaking cute. My heart is so full right now. I want to remember this moment for the rest of my life.

After texting Mom and checking in, I turn back to the bed and see both of my men sitting up, leaning back on the headboard. I'm suddenly aware of just how naked we all are. My dripping pussy is aware of that fact as well.

I lick my lips, trying to decide who I want inside of me first. Twenty-four hours ago, I was a virgin, and now, I'm pretty sure Jacob and Isaiah have made me addicted to sex. Or maybe it's just them I'm addicted to. Either way, I feel my pulse all the way down in my clit, throbbing and wanting more, more, *more*.

Crawling on the bed, I slowly make my way towards Isaiah, staring directly into his darkened eyes. I rip the sheet away from his lower half, exposing his massive cock. He fists himself, pumping up and down, but I slap his hand, making him growl.

Before he can protest, I straddle him, sliding down his cock, taking him into my pussy. He grabs my hips as I ride him. I hold onto his broad shoulders and use every single muscle in my body to fuck his big cock, riding him as hard as I can.

"Jesus, fuck, princess..." he groans, leaning forward and sucking on my nipple. I moan and arch my back, changing the angle so he rubs against my clit with every thrust.

"That's it, kitten, ride that fucking cock. Does it feel good, Nova? You like having him stretch you out while I watch?"

"Yes...God yes," I say on a shaky breath. My legs start to tremble, my whole body tense as I lift myself up and impale myself on Isaiah's dick again and again.

I hear Jacob moving around, and then I feel his body heat behind me. Jacob leans down and kisses my neck, sucking on my sensitive skin and biting me gently. I cry out and grind my pussy down harder, faster, seeking the release my body so desperately needs. Isaiah grunts and grabs my hips in a bruising grip, stilling my movements so he can fuck up into me.

Jacob cups my breasts and twists my nipples, kissing down my neck and rubbing his hard cock against my ass to get the friction he needs.

"Y-yes... Oh-ohmygod, yes," I stutter out.

My body locks up tightly, my breath catches in my throat, and my head tips back as I grunt and moan out my pleasure. Jacob trails a hand down my stomach and circles my clit with two fingers.

"Cum for us, kitten. Cum for us so hard, so fucking hard," Jacob murmurs into the shell of my ear before licking me there and trailing open-mouthed kisses up and down my neck.

I'm strung so tight, each of my men catering to my every need, fucking me, sucking me, stretching me, possessing me completely. Isaiah slams into me as Jacob pinches my clit and bites my shoulder. I'm trapped on the sharp edge of ecstasy, more, more, more, again, again, overwhelming pleasure bites into me, cutting through my core, and splitting me wide open.

I scream as I fly over the edge, free-falling into my orgasm. My pussy snaps around Isaiah's cock and a flood of wetness spills out of me like a dam bursting. I can't stop. My whole body spasms as I dig my nails into Isaiah's shoulders, needing to ground myself in some way. Jacob wraps his arms around my torso, holding me tight and not letting go while I ride out the endless waves of bliss.

Isaiah roars and then takes my lips in a punishing kiss. I feel him swell up inside of me and then his hot seed spills into my pussy as he rocks my body on top of his, finishing on a groan.

I rest my forehead on Isaiah's, both of us panting and shaking. "Fucking incredible," he whispers, kissing me again, softly this time.

I barely have time to nod my head in agreement before I'm being pulled off Isaiah's lap and tossed onto the mattress, landing on my back. Jacob crawls on top of me, spreading my legs wide open so he can settle his dick on top of my wet slit. He slides his monster cock through my folds, tapping the head of his cock on my clit and making my whole body twitch with each thrust.

"So damn sexy, Nova. Love your claws, kitten. Show them to me, show me how fierce you are."

With that, Jacob pulls back and rams his thick cock into my cunt, hitting home in one hard thrust. I scream and clench around him, wrapping my legs around his waist and my hands around his back.

Jacob scrapes his teeth down my neck, my collarbone, and over the tops of my breasts. I arch my back, taking him deeper as he pounds into me. He shows no mercy, fucking me so damn rough as he licks up my sweat and litters my skin with love bites. I want his mark, crave it with every cell in my body.

The sting of his teeth sets me on edge already, and I thrash around underneath him, clawing his back and digging my heels into his ass.

"Fuck yes, kitten, that's it, tear me up, beautiful," Jacob growls, picking up speed, fucking me into the mattress. I rake my nails across his skin, needing to mark him too. He responds by dropping his forehead to mine and grunting with each powerful thrust.

My orgasm slams into me, siphoning the air from my lungs and the strength from my body. Jacob pulls out and flips me over on my stomach, grabbing my hips and pulling my ass towards him.

"Again," he barks out, spreading my cheeks open and thrusting into my swollen, sensitive pussy. A jagged moan leaves my throat as I push myself up on shaky arms. I look over my shoulder at Jacob, who is staring at where we are connected.

He snaps his head up, staring right at me as he hammers into my little cunt again and again. He looks absolutely feral, grinding and rutting and tearing me up in the best way possible.

I feel a hand on my chin, guiding my face forward. I look up and see Isaiah kneeling in front of me, his cock already hard and leaking precum from the tip. My tongue automatically slips out of my mouth and I lick the drop right up, swallowing down his salty essence.

"Do you see what you do to me, princess? What you do to my cock? I swear the fucker is going to fall off from fucking all of your tight holes."

I moan and open up my mouth, letting him slide his rock-hard shaft past my lips. I massage the large, throbbing vein that runs along the bottom, loving the way he grunts with every swipe of my tongue.

Isaiah pulls back and threads his fingers in my hair, holding my head in place. He drags the tip of his dick around my lips, teasing me and making me crave him even more. His cock is wet with my saliva as well as his salty cum. I know my cum is on there as well, the dirty thought making me moan and clench my pussy up tight. Jacob grunts behind me and reaches out to play with my tits.

"Gonna fuck this pretty little mouth now, princess. You take what I give you, do you understand?"

I nod my head. Isaiah looks up at Jacob, who promptly slaps my ass. I gasp, and he does it again, harder. I arch my pack and press back into Jacob, wanting him to smack me again. I don't have time to be self-conscious about these twisted urges and desires. The need for my men is too great.

"He asked you a question, Nova. Answer him," Jacob growls.

"Yes, yes, fuck me, I'll take it, I'll take it all," I cry out.

Isaiah grunts in satisfaction and tightens his grip on my hair, pulling until it hurts so damn good. I open my mouth wide for him, showing him how much I want it. Isaiah slowly slides his cock inside and then backs out just as slow.

Then he snaps his hips and thrusts his cock inside of me, hitting the back of my throat and making my eyes water. I choke on his dick, gagging and crying and loving every second. Jacob pounds into me from behind while Isaiah fucks my mouth just like he promised he would.

I'm completely under their control, two cocks filling me up, using my body for their pleasure. I feel so sexy, so wanted, and despite the hard fuck they are giving me, I feel precious. Jacob and Isaiah are dominating me in the best way possible, and yet I feel like the powerful one.

Isaiah pulls out of me and I gasp for air. He tugs on my hair, tilting my head up so he can kiss me. "So good, sweet girl," he whispers into my parted lips. "So perfect. A perfect little fuck toy."

I should feel degraded, right? But his words spark a fire inside of me, one that has been building and building. It flares up and takes over my body when Isaiah bites my bottom lip and kisses me again, forcefully this time.

Jacob growls and slaps my ass again, hammering into me in sloppy, uneven thrusts. I feel him still and then burst inside of me. I surrender to the inferno deep in my belly, letting my orgasm burn through me and swallow me whole.

When I come back down from my high, I feel Jacob pull out, leaving me staring at Isaiah's angry-looking cock. I open my mouth again, taking him deep into my throat. He groans as I suck him down, wanting him to fill me up as well.

I feel Jacob's breath on my lower back, and then his lips press down over my spine. He trails soft kisses up my spine and strokes his hands up and down my sides, tracing my curves with his calloused fingers.

The mix of tender caresses and rough thrusts has me tensing up, shaking, overwhelmed, and over-sensitized. Every touch sparks my nerves, pain mixing with pleasure until I look up at Isaiah and plead with my eyes for him to cum.

He cups my face in his hands and looks at me with equal parts lust and adoration. One last thrust into my throat and I swallow around him, sucking his orgasm from his massive, swollen cock. He holds himself inside of me, shooting rope after rope down my throat while I swallow all of him.

Jacob grazes my clit with his finger, and that's all it takes.

I pop off Isaiah as my orgasm rips through me. I fall onto the bed and curl up in a ball, tensing, releasing, trembling, whimpering, and wet. So, so wet. Sweat, cum, and tears coat my body.

I'm vaguely aware of being lifted up and repositioned. When I open my eyes, I see Jacob looking down at me, his green eyes full of wonder, tinged with concern. I'm curled up in his lap, while Isaiah sits next to me, rubbing my back in calming circles and nuzzling into my neck.

"Talk to us, Nova. Was that okay? Are you okay?" Jacob asks.

I hold eye contact with him, so he can see my truth. "It was so good. You make me feel...free. Uninhibited. I didn't know I was into all of this, but I love it. I love when you're controlling me. I love everything you do to me. Both of you."

"Thank fuck," Jacob breathes out, pressing his lips to my forehead and leaving them there, breathing me in and rocking me back and forth.

"I also love this," I whisper, snuggling deeper into his chest.

"I love it too, beautiful," he murmurs.

"Me too," Isaiah mumbles, making me giggle.

We stay like that for a while, and then Isaiah picks me up off Jacob's lap so he can have his turn holding me. Being with these two is better than anything I could have ever dreamed of. If I wasn't sure before, this morning sealed the deal. They have my heart. I just hope they take care of it as well as they've been taking care of me.

Chapter 12

Jacob

The last four weeks have been the best of my life. I didn't know what I was missing until Nova showed up and stole my heart without even trying. She's given me all of her in return, her trust, her body, her goddamn soul. I know she loves us, even though she hasn't said it yet. None of us have.

I plan to change that tonight. I have a feeling Isaiah is waiting for me to make the first move, and I'm fine with that. If it means we can all get on the same page and start planning for the future, then I'm all for it. Because fuck yeah, now that I know what life with Nova is like, I'm never going back.

I never imagined sharing a woman in a real, honest to God relationship with Isaiah. I've never been in a real relationship, but then again, neither has Nova. Isaiah's only experience was getting his heart stomped on. I love that we're starting something new, something special together.

Nova has been busy this last week with work and several follow-up appointments for Miranda. So far, it's all been good news, which I know is a huge relief for Nova. For Isaiah and me as well. We don't just care because Miranda is Nova's mom, either. Nova has us over for dinner on Sunday nights, and we've had Miranda out here on the ranch as well. She loves the wide-open spaces and brushing the horses. She's not strong enough to ride yet, but I promised to give her a lesson when she's all healed.

Isaiah is opening up a little more day by day. I know he loves her, too. He's so completely devoted to her it's almost funny to watch. The quiet, broody, bastard with resting bitch face and ink crawling up his arms turns to complete mush whenever Nova is around.

I'd make fun of him if I weren't exactly the same way. Granted, it's not that much of a stretch for me. I'm not complicated or jaded like

Isaiah. I'm a simple man who has found love and happiness, and I'm smart enough to know I need to lock it down.

We're on our way to McLeon's Hardware store to meet Nova. She's working on another project for her mom - a porch swing this time. Isaiah and I have been helping her out with little home improvement projects as much as we can. Since our schedules are so busy, the only time we get to see each other during the week is when we're running errands or helping Nova with her projects. I'm hoping that will change tonight. Or, at least we'll start to build a future where we see each other more often. Preferably every night when we go to sleep and every morning when we wake up. As I said, I've got big plans for all of us, even if they don't know it yet.

Isaiah pulls into the parking lot, parking right next to Nova's old beat-up truck. She's leaning against the tailgate, beaming at us. Fuck, her smile gets me every single time. She's this intense, wild animal in bed and a total sweetheart in every other area of her life.

I smile to myself, remembering what Isaiah told Nova that first night we were all together. Apparently, he calls her *sweet girl* sometimes. It's their thing, just for them. I want that for him, for both of them. There's no jealousy. None at all. I know Isaiah needs that and I'm happy to pretend I was sleeping the whole time and didn't hear their conversation. I'll go the rest of my life turning a blind eye to it if it means I'll have both of them by my side the whole time.

"What's got you smiling so big?" Nova asks, walking up to me and resting her palms on my chest. I pull her close and give her a quick kiss, grinning when she pouts. We both know if I deepened the kiss, we'd end up fucking in the back of the truck in broad daylight. Honestly, I think Nova might be into trying it sometime. Our girl is kinky as fuck and I love every second.

"Just thinking about you, beautiful," I tell her. She rolls her eyes, but that smile is still shining through.

Nova pats my chest and spins around in my arms so she can hug Isaiah. He kisses the top of her head and takes her hand. I grab her other and we walk inside together. I wasn't sure how it would all play out, all three of us in public like this, but Nova has never once been ashamed of us or shy about giving us affection. I love that about her. About us. Fuck the world, we have each other.

We split up, each tackling a different part of the store with our lists in hand. The less time we spend at the store, the sooner we can work on the porch swing, which means we'll have more alone time with Nova once Miranda goes to bed.

I'm about half-way through the items on my list for the various other projects Isaiah and I have to do around the ranch when I spot Nova down the next aisle.

Some dipshit is standing much too close to our girl, and I can tell by his stance he's all wound up and aggressive. Nova's shoulders are squared, and her chin is stuck out in defiance. I know she's strong and independent, but that doesn't mean I don't have the urge to take care of her every second of every day.

"Hey, asshole, back the fuck up," I growl once I reach the two of them. Relief floods Nova's eyes, and I want to yank her into my chest and protect her from every bad thing. Unfortunately, Dipshit is standing between me and my woman.

He turns towards me with narrowed eyes and what I'm guessing is supposed to be an intimidating scowl. As soon as he sees how big I am, he changes his tune real quick. Instead of attempting to scare me off, he smirks and holds his hands up in surrender.

"Woah, no need to get violent or anything," Dipshit says. He looks familiar. Where have I seen his weaselly eyes and pointed nose before?

"Go away, Tim," Nova seethes, balling her hands into tiny fists. They wouldn't hurt this Tim asshole, but I love her fight and determination.

"Sure, sure, no worries," he agrees, though his tone of voice lets me know he'll continue to be a problem until I beat some sense into him.

He steps to the side and looks over my shoulder, his thin lips twisting up into an ugly, evil smile.

"What's going on here?" Isaiah's voice booms from behind me.

"He was just leaving," Nova says, shooting daggers at the moron who thought he could mess with my kitten.

Tim nods and slowly turns around, taking a few steps away from us. I'm about to pull Nova into my arms when he looks over his shoulder at us.

"For the record, I was just thanking your girl for a wild night. She took three of us on at once. Such a good little whore, aren't you, Nova? Call me if you want to do it again."

I roar and lunge for the fucker, but Nova grabs my arm and pulls me back. Tim sprints away from us, and it takes every goddamn thing in me not to chase after him. Nova's tight grip on my wrist is the only thing holding me back. That, and the fact that this is a small-ass town, so I know how to find the dead man and finish what we started.

I take a cleansing breath and turn to face Nova, who has unshed tears in her eyes.

"He's lying," she chokes out, the tears spilling over. "He's lying," she says again, looking over at Isaiah, who hasn't said a damn thing.

I look over at him as well, surprised he isn't going after Dipshit. What I see makes my blood boil. He's indifferent. No emotion. No anger on her behalf, no concern that she was just cornered and harassed. There's not even hurt in his eyes, though I know that's what he's really feeling.

"We know, kitten. Of course, he's lying."

She nods at me, looking a little more settled that at least one of us believes her. I elbow Isaiah in the ribs. Hard. But he doesn't budge. Nova looks over at him, pleading with her eyes for him to believe her too.

"I swear, I haven't been with anyone else. When would I even have the time? He's a jerk from high school, he's had it out for me for years, but I don't know why. I'm so sorry, Isaiah, you have to believe me, Tim is—"

"It doesn't matter," he cuts her off.

"What the fuck?" I say, pushing him back a bit. How fucking dare he make Nova feel bad about this.

Isaiah just shrugs, his eyes cold and trained right on Nova. "We were just fucking around, right? No hard feelings."

My jaw literally drops open as I gape after him. Isaiah walks away. He fucking walks away. I don't... I don't even know how to respond to that. I want to punch him. Knock some fucking sense into him. But I also want to comfort Nova, who is completely innocent. Never, not for even one second would I believe she's capable of cheating.

I know Isaiah is lashing out, speaking from that broken place, that wound he still carries deep inside his heart. That's no excuse for how he treated Nova.

"Jacob," Nova whispers, hiccupping miserably and trembling. "I'm sorry." She turns around and starts walking away as well.

I realize my silence and brief hesitation has given Nova the wrong idea. "Wait!" I call out after her. "Nova, stop!"

She spins on her heel and narrows her eyes at me. "Shh," she hisses. "We're making a scene."

"I don't care, I—"

"Well, I do. I can't be here right now, I'll...I'll talk to you later."

I look back over my shoulder, hoping, praying that Isaiah came to his senses and will come back here to grovel at Nova's feet. When I don't see him, I start following Nova towards the exit, needing to finish this conversation right the fuck now. If she wants to do it outside, so be it.

Just then, the security alarm goes off and several workers head in my direction. I realize I have an arm full of tools and materials, which must have set off the alarm when I tried to exit. I drop the items on the ground and run outside, only to see Nova gunning it out of the parking lot.

"Shit!" I yell, grabbing my hat and throwing it on the ground before raking my fingers through my hair, pulling at the strands in frustration.

I pull oxygen into my lungs, not even realizing I had stopped breathing for a second. Nova is as vital to my existence as air, and fucking Isaiah is ruining everything. I ball up my fists, every muscle in my body primed for the fight I never got with Tim.

As much as I want to destroy Isaiah right now, I have to keep it together. For Nova. I know she loves him and if I hurt him, she'd be even more hurt and conflicted than she is right now. I love Isaiah, too. He's my twin for fuck's sake. I just need to figure out a way to fix what he broke and make sure he never pulls this kind of shit again.

I storm over to the truck where Isaiah is sitting in the driver seat, his face tight with all the emotion he's trying not to show. I wrench the passenger side door open and bite back the need to rip my twin brother to shreds.

We drive back to the ranch without saying a single word to each other. It's the loudest silence I've ever experienced.

When we pull into the property, Knox and Noah are sitting on the front porch, shooting the shit. They give us a weird look, no doubt wondering why we're here instead of with Nova like we planned.

Isaiah throws the truck in park and stomps towards our cabin, ignoring the greeting Knox gives him. Noah has seen Isaiah in one of his moods before, so he doesn't bother saying anything to him.

I blow out a tension-filled breath and walk up to the porch. If Isaiah is going to be in the cabin, then I need to be somewhere else. I can't fucking look at him right now.

"What the hell happened?" Knox asks diving right into the conversation.

"Old demons die hard," I mutter, taking the beer Noah offers gratefully.

"Everything alright with Nova?" Noah asks.

I sigh and wipe a hand down my face. I'm thankful that everyone here at the ranch accepted the three of us without so much as a raised eyebrow. I know our relationship is far from traditional but having the people I call family welcome Nova into their lives means everything to me. It's just one more sign that this is all meant to be. I just have to figure a way out of this mess.

"Not really," I start, taking a sip of my beer. "We were at the store when some asshat cornered her. I scared him off, but not before he threw some awful accusations out, called her..." I growl and ball my fists up remembering what Tim said about my kitten.

"Alright, so he was an asshole and an idiot. Is Nova alright?" Knox asks.

"Yeah, I mean, the guy didn't touch her, or else he'd be a dead motherfucker. But Isaiah..." I trail off and shake my head before gulping down the rest of my beer. I tell them about Isaiah's ex and how poorly he handled everything with Nova at the store.

Noah has been silent this whole time, but I know he has something to say. He and Jade went through something similar when they first got together. Knox seems to sense the same thing because he stops peppering me with questions and looks over at his best friend.

Noah clears his throat and looks straight ahead, over the gorgeous rolling hills of the ranch. "I guarantee that Isaiah already regrets his actions. He knows deep down, under all that pain and shame, that Nova isn't his ex. But once someone breaks your trust like that... Damn, it's hard not to see that in everyone, even those you love."

"So what do I do? Talk to him? Leave him alone? What about Nova? She made it clear she wants space, but I sure as fuck don't."

"You know Isaiah better than I do," Noah answers. "But I think he needs a day or two to get his shit straight. He's probably feeling a lot of shame and anger. He's mad at himself and he's probably thinking that he can't trust anyone, especially himself."

I grunt in acknowledgment. "Yeah, he told me the same thing after the stuff with his ex went down. But he has me, he has Nova, we have a good thing going. The best thing. How can he throw that all away?"

Knox grabs us another round of beers and hands them out while Noah contemplates my question. I'm hanging on his every word. I want to understand Isaiah so badly, I want him to finally get past this so we can get our girl back.

I get frustrated all over again thinking about how I was finally going to tell Nova I love her. I long to hear her say those words back to me, to us. I thought maybe once Isaiah heard it too, he could let go of that last thread of doubt holding him back. And then fucking dipshit Tim ruined everything.

"If Isaiah is anything like me, the past and the pain is blinding him to how his actions have affected others. He's being a selfish ass, but in his head, he probably thinks he's sacrificing his happiness so Nova can be happy. And not that I know a damn thing about all y'alls relationship, but I'd bet the ranch he's thinking you and Nova would be happy together without him."

"Who is betting my ranch?" Jade, Noah's wife, asks as she swings the front door open. Her eyes light up when she sees Noah. He reaches out and pulls her to his side, kissing the top of her head.

"Just giving some relationship advice," Noah says.

"Uh-oh. Better let me help," Jade teases. Once she sees my face, however, she sobers up. "Something going on with you, Nova, and Isaiah?"

I nod and give her the short version of what happened. I don't love telling everyone my shit, but I'm at a loss, and lord knows Isaiah is not going to be any help in this situation.

"Teagan and I will take her out for a girls' night! I've been dying to get to know Nova better anyway. I'm sure Teagan wouldn't mind a night off from mommy duty, right Knox?" Jade gives him a stern look that would make anyone submit to her request.

"Yes, great idea," he's quick to agree. "How about Friday? I'll cook dinner while you and Teagan take Nova out."

"Friday?" I question. "That's five days from now. How the hell am I supposed to survive that long without her?"

Jade gives me a sad, understanding look. "I know you love her, Jacob. Y'all are good together, and I really think you can get past this, but she needs some space. You don't want to crowd her while she still has stuff going on with Miranda and working her ass off at Roy's. I promise your girl is in good hands, okay?"

I nod and finish my beer, thanking my friends for listening and stepping in. Some might think it's intrusive or nosy, but I couldn't be more grateful for these people.

Chapter 13

Nova

What a fucking week.

I've been pulling double shifts these last few days since one of the other waitresses got the flu. Honestly, I'm glad for the distraction. Not that I'm not thinking about Jacob and Isaiah every minute of every day, but at least when I'm at work I'm *doing* something. As opposed to when I'm thinking about them at home and crying into my pillow.

"Thanks again for covering, Nova," Sarah, my boss, says. "You can head out a few minutes early, I know you've had a long day."

I nod my thanks and go to the backroom to gather my things. A long day indeed. The longest. Especially considering what I found out this morning.

Shaking my head of those thoughts, I make my way out to the back lot where employees park. As soon as I step outside, the hair on the back of my neck stands up. It's quiet. The air is still. Nothing is out of place. And yet...something is wrong.

I linger in the doorway for a split second, looking over my shoulder into the diner. A huge group of high schoolers getting out of the home football game just came through the doors. I know if I go back, I'll be sticking around for at least another two hours, and my feet cannot handle that. Plus, what would I say, anyway? Nothing is happening. But it still feels off.

Digging around in my purse, I fumble for my keys and pepper spray. A girl can't be too careful these days. I take a deep breath and head out to my truck, which, unfortunately, is in the second to last parking spot at the far end of the lot.

I make my way there at a quick pace, but not running. My feet are too sore to run. Plus, I don't want to appear suspicious. Confidence is key, right? Or does that not apply to this situation? I don't know. I'm so damn tired.

By the time I reach my truck, I'm feeling pretty foolish. I'm not even sure what I thought was going to happen, I just felt...

"Finally," a familiar voice booms from the other side of my truck. Tim steps out from where he was hiding, along with his two asshole lackeys. "You were in there for fucking ever. I hope you're not too worn out to pay up," he says, a sickening laugh bubbling up from his throat.

"Excuse me?" I snap. I'm so done with this shit. "Pay up? Who the fuck do you think you are? Why are you doing this to me? I thought I was the fat cow, the disgusting lump no one would love. What changed since high school, huh?"

When my rant is over, I take a large gulp of air and fix my gaze on Tim, demanding answers.

He throws his head back and laughs. Cackles, really. I hate the sound.

"Nova, *you* changed. You grew into your curves, I guess. Or maybe I just got tired of fucking skinny bitches and wanted to see what all the fuss was about you. I mean, you snagged twins, so you must have a magic pussy."

"Fuck you, Tim. I'm not yours, get the hell away from me and go suck off Tweedledee and Tweedledum over there," I say, nodding to his pathetic friends who haven't said a single word this whole time.

Wrong move. Tim closes the distance between us in two strides, his eyes burning with rage. I quickly turn around and shove my key into the door of the truck, cursing the thing for the first time ever. If I had a newer truck, I could have unlocked the door with a button and already be running over these douchebags.

"You'll pay for that, too, bitch," Tim snarls from right behind me. I feel his breath on the back of my neck. It's almost as tangible as the anger that's coming off him in waves. "Your *boyfriends* made me look like a fool that night you were hanging out here at Roy's. I lost a date over it. And then when I saw you at the hardware store, they jumped down my throat again. They aren't better than me, you know. If they can have you, then so can I."

I bite back the litany of responses to all of his sexist, degrading, idiotic remarks. Right now, I need to focus on getting the hell out of here. It's not just me I have to worry about anymore.

With one hand still wrapped around my pepper spray, and one hand gripping my keys, I spin around and elbow Tim, catching him off guard. He stumbles back a bit, giving me enough room to adjust my keys so each one is sticking out from in between my clenched fingers.

He's still in shock, so I make my move. I lunge at him with my fist cocked and land a blow to his cheek. He screeches pathetically and falls backward. I don't have much time to enjoy my victory, however. The two dingbats come at me, but I'm prepared. I hold out the pepper spray and am about to let them have it when Jacob and Isaiah come running up out of nowhere.

Jacob grabs one guy and decks him in the mouth before picking him up by his collar and tossing him on the ground a few feet away. Isaiah does pretty much the same to the other guy. The two morons scamper off, abandoning their leader.

Jacob and Isaiah turn their attention on Tim, who is curled up in a ball, pretending to be dead or something. Figures. Jacob looks like he's going to murder the asshole, so I step in. As much as I want to see Tim get everything that's coming to him, I don't want to be here to witness it. If my men find him later and beat his ass, that's on them.

My men.

The thought twists my gut, making my heart squeeze up painfully in my chest.

"Stop!" I yell, my voice weaker than I'd like to admit. "Stop, he's not worth jail time."

Jacob and Isaiah snap their heads towards me. Tim even pops an eye open. Fucking moron.

"Kitten, I can't let him get away with this shit again. I'm gonna need a better reason than jail time to not end this motherfucker right now," Jacob grits out. Isaiah snarls his agreement.

"I—"

My words are cut off when Tim tries to crawl away and Isaiah lands a kick to his stomach. Tim sputters and coughs, then holds his hands up in surrender.

"My bad, won't happen again, she's all yours," he pleads.

Jacob cracks a fist on Tim's face, laying him out flat.

"Sorry, kitten," he mumbles after spitting on the now unconscious body of my would-be attacker. "I had to. No honorable man would let someone treat a woman that way, let alone their woman."

I bark out a bitter laugh, my hands shaking as the adrenaline leaves my body. "Your woman? How about you, Isaiah? Am I yours too?"

Isaiah doesn't say anything. His face is totally blank, much like the last time I saw him. How can I mean nothing to him? We shared so much, not just our bodies, but our hearts, our thoughts, our Sunday evenings, and every other evening we had free. We were building a life, or at least I was. It hurt beyond words that he took Tim's word over mine without even letting me explain. His words echo in my head every single day, all day long.

We were just fucking around, right? No hard feelings.

Just fucking around. Just. Fucking. Around.

It's not true. It can't be true. I know it's not true for Jacob, but I can't even begin to imagine a life without Isaiah. It's not that I don't love Jacob, but I would never be complete without both of them. It's all or nothing, it always has been.

"Nova, are you okay? Are you hurt?" Jacob asks softly from right next to me. I didn't realize how close he'd gotten while I was staring at Isaiah's impassive face. He's brutally handsome and I miss him so much I can hardly breathe. I tear my eyes away from Isaiah and look at Jacob.

Where Isaiah's gaze was cold and indifferent, Jacob's is full of emotion and warmth. Sadness, worry, but also relief. Seeing him like this hurts just as much as Isaiah's silence. Knowing I can't have one without the other. I can't have Jacob's sweetness, and being in his presence only makes it harder.

"Why are you here?" I ask, hardening my voice. Darting my eyes over to Isaiah, I repeat, "Why the *fuck* are you here? It was pretty clear you only wanted to fuck around, and I hate to break it to you, but I'm not up for that tonight."

Isaiah clenches his jaw, but he doesn't break. I do.

I slump against the truck as tears spill out of my eyes. I wipe them away, frustrated at my own weakness.

"Can you tell us what happened? Do you need to go to the hospital?" Jacob asks.

"I'm fine," I say through pathetic tears. "He didn't touch me. I had everything handled without you two. I took Tim out, I was gonna pepper spray the other two, I'm fine. I was going to take care of it like I do everything."

Jacob looks like I slapped him. I hate that I'm hurting him too, but I just need to get out of here. I have a girls' night with Teagan and Jade tomorrow, and I've already decided that will be my last goodbye to them. There's no way I can hang around anyone from Rivera Ranch without being constantly reminded of what I almost had. A big, welcoming family. Friends. Little ones running around.

Another sob shudders through my body, and I clamp my hand over my mouth to muffle the sound, dropping my keys in the process.

Jacob reaches out for me, but I flinch away. He looks so hurt, but I am too. I need to leave, and soon. I'm crashing, hard, and I just want to take a hot shower and cry myself to sleep.

"Kitten..."

I shake my head and try to gather my wits. I survived everything else tonight, I just need to get home. I push off the side of the truck and bend down to grab my keys, but the world tilts a bit and my vision goes spotty. Jacob wraps his big, strong arms around me and pulls me into his chest.

"Please," I whimper, closing my eyes.

"Please, what, beautiful?" Jacob whispers, resting his forehead on mine.

"Please let me go. I can't...I can't... He doesn't love me." It's barely a whisper, and I'm not even sure Jacob heard me.

"I'm not letting you go. Isaiah is a fucking dumbass—"

Isaiah growls in the background. I find myself crying and yet smiling at the same time. It hurts so damn much.

"Dumb. Ass," Jacob repeats louder. "But we love you. We love you so much, please let me beat Isaiah up and then let him beg for your forgiveness."

"He doesn't want me."

Jacob tilts his head up, looking to the sky as if asking for strength. Then he looks over his shoulder and glares in Isaiah's direction. "Dude, stop being a coward and come tell our girl how much of a colossal bag of dicks you are and how you'll do anything to be worthy of licking the ground she walks on. This is it, man, this is the rest of your life you're screwing up. And mine. And Nova's."

I hear heavy footsteps and my heart stupidly leaps in my chest. I'm mad at Isaiah. I want him to suffer like I've been suffering. I want to yell at him and ask how he could throw everything away, how he could make me fall madly in love with him, and then just walk out on me. I want to slap him and kiss him and fuck him and then yell at him some more.

He's right behind me. His shadow falls over me, his scent wraps around me, and I can't help but turn around in Jacob's arms. The motion messes with me, setting me off balance.

The ground slips from underneath me and my vision goes blurry. My entire body heats up and then I go ice cold. I hear my heart pounding, the blood rushing in my ears. My men are calling for me, but I'm already underwater, sinking down, down, down into the darkness. The last thing I see is Isaiah's dark green eyes filled with tears.

Chapter 14

I'm an idiot. A dumb ass. A colossal bag of dicks, just like Jacob has been telling me all week.

I grunt in frustration and rub my hands up and down my face before gripping my hair and tugging at the strands until it hurts. Pacing around outside of the hospital and muttering to myself, I'm sure I look like a fucking lunatic on top of everything else.

Nova, *our Nova*, is inside getting checked out after fainting in my arms. I'll never forget the panicked look in her whiskey-colored eyes. The depth of pain, of betrayal, of complete disbelief that I'd catch her when she fell. Never again. Never, ever again will I put that look in my woman's eyes.

Fuck, I've been so blind these last few days. I lost my shit when I heard the accusations thrown at Nova, and I handled the situation in the worst way possible. All I heard when she opened her mouth to defend herself were excuses. *When would I have time to cheat? He's just someone I knew from high school.* And then there's the fact that she apologized. Only guilty people apologize.

Or so I thought in that state of mind. After taking some time to cool down, as well as being on the receiving end of Jacob's non-stop verbal abuse, I realize that Nova was apologizing because she knew the asshole's comments hurt me.

So fucking sweet. My sweet girl. My princess.

And I walked away from her.

In my hurt and embarrassment of that day, I didn't even realize how shook up Nova was about the whole incident. It wasn't until Jacob knocked some sense into me (again), that more and more pieces fell into place. This Tim character was the dude from the bar. The one who bullied Nova in high school. The same soon-to-be-dead motherfucker who attacked her earlier tonight.

I hate myself for letting this happen. On some level, I know Tim's actions are his responsibility and his alone, but I can't help but think this wouldn't have happened if I wasn't such an asshole. Jacob and I would have taken out the fucker long before today. We would have made it clear that Nova was off-limits. Instead, I broke us, broke what we had. I threw away everything because I couldn't get over my past.

When I saw Nova again tonight, my heart stuttered in my chest and my insides twisted up tight. It was more than anger at the three men intimidating her, it was the fact that I haven't been able to breathe all week until I was in her presence.

Shame and self-loathing flooded my system, and I took my anger out on her attackers. I would have beaten each of them into a bloody, mangled pulp, but Nova didn't want that, and I will never be in a position to deny her anything for the rest of our lives.

I could barely stand to look at her without crying, and when our eyes finally did meet, I had to school my face over to keep from giving away all of my emotions. I had been planning on walking away again, letting her and Jacob start over, start something without me. It was only fair to both of them. I fucked up, so I should go away. No need for me to stain an otherwise beautiful relationship and life.

But then Jacob put me in my place in the way only he can. Nova even seemed like she might consider allowing me to apologize before she fainted.

Fuck. The moment she went down, my arms were around her, cradling her close. That was it. Nothing else matters but having her in my arms for all of time. Whatever it takes, I'll prove to Nova I love her with all of me and I'll never leave her again.

I growl and punch the wall in frustration, letting the brick scrape against my knuckles and rip up my skin. I want the pain. The bruises. The blood. I deserve it.

I wind up for another punch, but Jacob walks out the side door, heading straight towards me. There's a glint of dangerous anger in his eyes, and I know before he reaches me what's going to happen. I turn to face him and brace for the impact of his fist. I deserve it.

He hits me square in the jaw, sending me tumbling to the ground. Jacob towers over me, gritting his teeth and clenching his fists. "Get up, fucker," he spits out.

Standing up right in front of him, I let him know I'm ready for the next hit. Instead, Jacob takes a huge breath and lets it out, deflating against the wall of the hospital. He rubs his closed eyes with his fingers while taking another breath. I stand in silence, waiting for him to speak first.

Jacob opens his eyes, hitting me with a look of defeat and wariness that hurts worse than any sucker punch could. I've not only hurt the love of my life, but I've hurt my best friend, my twin, the man who has always been there for me.

I want to apologize, fuck, I want to cry, but I keep it in. I wait for him to let me have it. I deserve his harsh truths, his fists, his abandonment if that's what he chooses to do.

"I'm nothing without her," he whispers, more to himself than to me.

I nod, silently letting him know I'm right there with him. Nova makes me someone worth loving. Without her, I'm a bitter, grumpy, shell of a man. I know beyond a shadow of a doubt I'll be empty forever unless she forgives me.

"You have to make this right," Jacob says, addressing me this time.

I nod in agreement.

"It's not just you, here, it's me, too. She wants us both or nothing at all. There are no favorites. Do realize how fucking rare that is?"

Again, I nod.

"What the hell, Iz? Show some goddamn emotion! I'm a fucking wreck. I want to murder those degenerates, and honestly, I want to murder you a little bit, too. I'm scared out of my mind for our girl, I'm hurting so bad it feels like I can't breathe. I'm exhausted. I'm a mess.

And you? You stand there stoic as ever. Does this mean nothing?" He throws his hands in the air, motioning towards everything around him.

"I..." My words die in my throat. What do I even say to that?

"Seriously? Come on, man, give me something. How are you this impassive? We were on our way to get our girl back, for Christ's sake, and then when we got to her, you froze. You had your shot and you blew it. Fucking blew it." He sighs, defeatedly. "I have nothing else to say, Iz. I know whatever is going on in your head is worse torture than anything I could dole out, so that's it. I'm done."

I open my mouth but then close it again when the side door swings open with a bang. Miranda steps out and heads our way. My heart is in my throat as I wait for her to tell us what happened. I have no idea how to even begin to beg for forgiveness from all of these people in my life, including Nova's mom.

"They are done with the tests. Everything is fine, Nova is healthy, just tired. She's resting now."

I release the breath that was trapped in my lungs, as does Jacob.

"Oh thank fuck," Jacob sighs in relief.

I swallow around the lump in my throat and nod. Because I'm an idiot who can't seem to do anything or show anything, even when it comes to the people I love.

"Can we see her?" Jacob asks.

Miranda eyes him up and down, before doing the same to me. She balls up one hand and puts it on her hip while pointing at us with her other hand. "I don't know what happened between the three of you, but if you ever, *ever* hurt my baby again, I will end you. I will cast every vengeful spell I know, perform every dark ritual I can get my hands on, pray to the Goddess herself to rain fire and destruction down on your lives. And if that doesn't work, I'll grab the shotgun I keep under my bed and pay both of you a visit, don't think I won't."

I believe every single word out of her mouth. This is where Nova gets her grit and determination. I just pray Jacob and I can stick around long enough to see more of it from both Nova and her mom.

Miranda continues, though most of the fierceness is gone from her words, replaced with a tender, motherly love. "I love that girl with my entire heart and all that is good within me. I've made my mistakes, and I didn't always know how to love her or what she needed from me. But I've never seen my honeykins more fulfilled, more confident, more joyful than when you three were together. You," she points to Jacob, "You are good at reminding Nova to lighten up and enjoy life. And you," she points to me, "You speak to her in that calming tone of yours that gets her to listen, *really* listen in a way she never has before. Both of you take such good care of her and make her feel safe and wanted. You better make her feel that way again. This is my one and only warning."

With that, she spins on her heel and walks back towards the hospital. Jacob shoots me a look full of determination. We're in this together. Even though I broke us, and despite his earlier words, I know he's going to help me get our Nova back.

Chapter 15

Nova

My head is fuzzy, and my limbs feel like stone. Stiff sheets scrape against my skin, reminding me that I'm in a hospital bed. After waking up the first time, the doctor on call ran the standard tests and had me on an IV drip to keep me hydrated. She told me to rest and then I could be discharged after another checkup. One of the nurses must have removed the IV because I don't feel the tug of the tape on my arm anymore.

I don't want to open my eyes just yet, so I take a deep breath and try to hold onto the feeling of being in Isaiah's arms when I fainted. I conjure up the way Jacob's forehead felt against mine, the way his breath tickled across my lips when he said he's not letting me go.

I must have a better imagination than I give myself credit for, because with each slow, measured breath in and out, I get a hint of sandalwood, along with pine and the smell right after a rainstorm. It smells like Jacob and Isaiah, and my heart hurts. I squeeze my eyes and hold my breath, trying not to let the tears escape.

"It's okay, kitten," I hear Jacob say from right beside me.

My eyes fly open and I let out a surprised squeak when I see warm, gentle green eyes stare back at me. Jacob leans forward and kisses my temple while running a warm, calloused hand up and down my exposed arm.

I want to throw myself in his arms and soak up whatever comfort he has to offer, but I restrain myself. I can't have Jacob without Isaiah.

As if on cue, I feel a second warm, calloused hand close around mine, and I turn to see Isaiah bring my hand up to his lips and brush a tender kiss over my knuckles. I can't stop the sob that escapes my lips. He tips his head up, searing me with all of the shame and regret in the world.

"Nova, I..." He closes his eyes, his face scrunching up in pain like it's physically hurting him to express himself. It tears at something deep inside of me. I don't want to be angry. I don't want to get revenge. I don't want to hurt anymore. I just want to be with my men, my twins, the two halves of my heart.

I place my hand on the side of his face, stroking my thumb over his cheek to encourage him to continue. I might not want revenge, but I deserve an apology. Isaiah turns his head to kiss my palm, then places my hand back on his cheek, covering it with his own.

"I'm so fucking sorry. No, sorry doesn't cover it. I... Nova, you... When... Fuck," he mutters, leaning back and breaking our connection.

"No!" I whimper, sitting up and reaching out for him. "Don't leave me."

Isaiah looks up at me, stricken by my words. Immediately, he returns to me, kneeling down and taking my face in his hands.

"Never, sweet girl. Never again," he whispers. "I fucked up. I didn't think, I just reacted when I heard that fucker say those things. I broke your trust, Nova, and for that, I can never apologize enough. I don't deserve forgiveness, but I'm asking anyway."

He kisses my forehead and then rests his on the same spot before continuing.

"I love you. I love you more than I thought possible, more than I ever thought I was capable of. You healed places inside of me I didn't even know were broken, and then I let my past, my insecurities ruin everything. Please, Nova, God, please heal me again. Save me from myself, and I swear to you, I'll save you from every goddamn thing in this world. I'll protect you with my last breath. I fucking love you. Please, just...please forgive me?"

Overwhelmed by his confession and the fact that this gigantic, rough cowboy is literally on his knees, begging for my forgiveness, I throw my arms around him and bury my face in his neck. "I forgive you. I love you too, you idiot," I mumble. I have to give him some shit, after all.

Isaiah pulls me back so he can see the truth in my eyes. "Tell me again, love. I need to hear it."

"I love you."

"The other part."

"I forgive you."

He closes his eyes, his deep, dark, beautiful green eyes. When he opens them again, I see nothing but love and adoration shining through. Isaiah tucks my hair behind my ear and wraps his hand around the back of my neck, pulling me closer. We're millimeters apart when he whispers, "I'll spend the rest of my life trying to be worthy of your love."

He seals his declaration with a kiss. It's so sweet, so reverent, so full of love, there's no way I could doubt his words.

We break apart only when I hear Jacob clear his throat. Isaiah reluctantly steps away from me, but not before kissing my forehead one last time.

When I look up at Jacob, he has his signature goofy, charming grin playing at his lips. I can't help but return his smile, though mine is a little waterier than his. "Told you he was a dumb ass."

I laugh and then hiccup out a few tears, overwhelmed in more ways than one. Jacob wipes my tears away and then kisses me soundly.

"Love you, beautiful. I have from day one. You're ours."

I nod and kiss him again. "I love you, too. So much. I'm sorry I hurt you. I couldn't—"

He places a finger over my lips to stop me. "Not another word, kitten. We're all here. We're together. That's all that matters. The three of us."

His words bring reality crashing into the surface of our little love bubble. Will they still want me when I tell them what I found out earlier today? Will this all just be one last cruel joke the universe plays on me before taking away my dreams?

"Hey," Jacob says, softly. "What is it? What's wrong?"

Immediately, Isaiah pops up from his seat and is right next to me.

"I, um… I need some air. Can you guys just…"

They step back, though I can tell it pains them to do so. I grab one of their hands with each of my own, lacing our fingers together. Blowing out a breath, steel my nerves and blurt out the news that might take everything away.

"I'm pregnant," I whisper, closing my eyes so I can hold on to the way they looked at me when they said they loved me. I might not get that ever again. They said we're all that matters, just the three of us. But what about four? How would that work? Would Isaiah be jealous and constantly wonder if the child is Jacob's and not his? Or vice versa? Do they even want kids?

Isaiah drops my hand and my heart sinks. I open my eyes and see him kneeling down in front of me again, only this time, he presses kisses over my belly.

"I'm one of your daddies," he says on a shaky breath. "I love you so much, little one. You and your mom. My whole world."

I run my fingers through Isaiah's hair, and he looks up at me with tears in his eyes. "Thank you, Nova. You've given me more than I deserve, more than I could ever have hoped for."

I smile and nod my head, taking a cue from my stoic, yet soulful cowboy. This is more than anything I could have ever hoped for, too.

Jacob squeezes my hand, causing me to look up at him. He's full-on cry-smiling, always one to express his emotions freely. It makes me want to be open with mine as well, even the doubtful ones.

"Can we make this work? Where will we stay? Whose name is going to go on the birth certificate? I want this family with you both so bad it hurts, but I'm afraid it's all going to blow up in my face."

Isaiah wraps me up in his arms and then stands up, pulling me with him. I hang onto him tightly, though I know he'd never let me fall. Jacob comes up behind me, hugging both of us. "We'll do whatever you want, beautiful," Jacob says.

"I know you want the details all worked out, princess, and we'll get there," Isaiah says, the peaceful, familiar rumble of his voice calming me as only he can. "All that is important now is that you're healthy. You and our baby."

I sniffle and nod, letting the warmth of my men surround me. Something settles deep in my bones. The last of my worries and fears slip away.

"I love you both so much," I whisper.

"God, I love you," Jacob says, nuzzling into my shoulder.

"Love you, princess," Isaiah murmurs, rubbing his nose against mine.

I soak up all of their love and then wiggle out from between them. Taking one of their hands in each of mine, I lead us over to the couch, since I don't think the bed would support all three of us, unfortunately.

I look down at where my fingers are woven together with Isaiah's and am shocked to see dried blood. "Oh my God, Isaiah, is that from when you punched that guy tonight?"

He looks away from me and slips his hand from mine. "Uh, no, I sort of...had an altercation with a brick wall."

"You punched a wall?"

He nods and looks over at me. "I caused you pain," he explains. "I deserved to feel pain too."

My heart breaks for this man in front of me. He's got all of these layers and he has no idea how much I love him. "You can't hurt yourself without hurting me, too."

We stare at each other for a few moments, Isaiah taking in my love, my truth, while I absorb his pain and sorrow. I reach out and trace my fingertips over a red, swollen bump on his jaw, then tick my eyes over to Jacob.

"That goes for you too, mister," I narrow my eyes at him. "I'm guessing Isaiah didn't punch himself in the face?" Jacob doesn't confirm or deny my suspicions. "You can't hurt each other without hurting me. You're both my whole life, my heart."

"But he was being a selfish asshole!" Jacob whines. I almost grin at his pouty face, but I need him to hear me out.

"No more fighting. When we have problems, we talk them out, deal?" I glare at both of them, and they nod in unison. I can't help the smug smile that overtakes my face.

"You like knowing you command us, my queen?" Isaiah murmurs before kissing me.

"Yes, very much so," I sigh, resting my head on his shoulder. Isaiah kisses the top of my head while Jacob tucks my hair behind my ear and kisses my neck. Two large, protective hands rest on my belly. I lay my hands on top of theirs and feel the last piece of my heart snap into place, beating with the knowledge that my men will always be there for me like this.

Chapter 16

Jacob

"Where are you guys taking me?" Nova asks excitedly, bouncing on the bench seat between Isaiah and me in the truck.

"You're so impatient!" I tease, turning down the gravel road that winds around the outside of Rivera Ranch.

"You really aren't going to tell me?" She blinks up at me, batting her eyelashes. I grin and shake my head. Nova grumbles and then looks over at Isaiah, nudging him with her elbow. "And you? Just gonna leave me out here in the dark?"

He shrugs. "Who says I know where we're going?" Nova eyes him skeptically and shakes her head like she doesn't believe him.

"Should've figured you'd both team up on me," she mutters.

"You say that like it's a bad thing, kitten. I seem to remember a certain feisty, filthy-as-fuck woman who didn't mind being double-teamed not all that long ago."

"Oh my *God*!" Nova gasps, smacking my chest. "You can't just say stuff like that!"

"But it's so fun to see your face turn bright red." I wink at her, chuckling when her face grows even redder.

Nova turns to Isaiah again and crosses her arms over her chest. "You're not going to come to my defense at all, huh?"

Isaiah shrugs again. "Jacob's right. It *is* really fun to see your face turn bright red."

I laugh and then get smacked again. Grabbing Nova's hand, I lace our fingers together and set our joined hands on my lap. Isaiah does the same, holding her hand on his lap as well. Nova sighs and rests her head on my shoulder.

"Don't get too comfortable, princess. We'll be there soon."

She pops up and looks over at Isaiah, who gives her a knowing smirk. "So you *do* know where we're going!"

The man shrugs, making Nova growl and me laugh. I was worried it would take us a long time to get back to this place of shared laughter and easy banter, but Nova once again proved to be better than anything I could have ever hoped for.

She was released from the hospital two days ago and hasn't left our sides since. We took her home that night and drew her a bath, letting her soak while we helped Miranda off to bed and picked up around the house. When Nova came out of the tub, we took her straight to bed and curled up around her until we all fell asleep.

Nova got a few days off of work, so she hung out with us on the ranch yesterday and today, floating between me and Isaiah and then running up to the main house to talk to the girls about baby stuff.

Baby.

We're having a baby.

God, when she told us she was pregnant, I swear I almost fainted. No joke. It was the biggest rush of my life, knowing Nova, Isaiah, and I would be bound together forever. It killed me to see the doubt in her eyes like she thought we'd take back our love.

Isaiah nailed it though, sinking down on his knees in front of her. The man doesn't show emotion often, but when he does, he goes all in. If ever there were a time to lay all of his cards on the table, that was it, and he didn't hesitate this time.

"Whatcha thinking about?" Nova asks, pulling me back into the present.

"You," I tell her honestly. She rolls her eyes but then gives me one of her heart-stopping smiles. "You're so damn beautiful."

"Enough of that," she says, dismissing my compliment with a wave of her hand. I grip it and kiss her palm, unable to keep my hands or lips to myself for a single second.

"Fine, but only because we're here," I say in my most stern voice. Nova laughs, which is fair. Isaiah is the stern one, but it's nice to switch it up every once in a while.

"What a cute house! Who lives here?" Nova asks, bouncing out of the truck. Isaiah grips her hips and eases her down onto the ground.

"Easy now, princess. You can't be taking any tumbles, especially now that you're carrying my kid."

I can't see Nova, but I can practically hear her pout. "Mine too!" I shout out as I run around the truck and rest a palm over Nova's belly. She places her hand on mine and looks up at me with a watery smile. "Hey, what's with the tears, kitten?"

Nova sniffles and wipes away a tear that escaped her eye. "Both of you…I mean, would you ever want to find out? Like, who the dad is? Could they even determine that since you're both twins?"

"Oh, Nova," I whisper, hugging her into my chest. "Beautiful, that baby is mine. And Isaiah's. And yours. We don't need a test. What would that prove anyway?"

"You won't have your doubts?" she asks, turning in my arms to look at Isaiah. He immediately shakes his head no and cups her cheek.

"Never. Plus, I'm hoping for twins. It runs in the family, you know," Isaiah says, lifting an eyebrow at her.

Nova hiccups out a laugh and I join her.

Leaning down, I kiss Nova's temple before murmuring in her ear, "If we don't have twins this time, we'll just have to keep knocking you up until you do."

"Oh yeah? And where are we going to raise these many children you speak of?"

I can't help the grin that splits my face in two. "I was thinking we'd start right here, but when we have a baker's dozen of kids, we'll have to get a bigger place."

"What?!" Nova gasps cand looks at the house, really looks at it this time. Her mouth hangs wide open as she takes in the cute ranch-style house. She looks at me and then at Isaiah, and then back at me. "What?!" she asks again. "Where…when did you…wait, *what*?!"

Isaiah chuckles and grabs her hand, pulling her towards the house. I follow behind, producing the key to the front door and holding it open for them.

"I was going to show both of you last week when I put the deposit money and first and last month's rent down. But then...well, then we got a bit distracted, but we're here now and that's all that matters, right?"

Nova darts her eyes between Isaiah and me. "Last week? So you wanted to move in with me even before everything went down and before the pregnancy?"

"Of course," I say, wrapping an arm around her waist and pulling her into my side while I walk us around the place to give her a tour. "I knew you were ours and that we needed to take things to the next level. I would have moved you in after our first date, but that wouldn't have been right. Miranda needed you, we didn't really know each other, and it would have been ten kinds of wrong to ask you to move into our tiny cabin on the ranch. I did some digging and found this place for rent."

Nova still hasn't said anything, so I keep on rambling, nervous for her reaction. Did I just fuck this up? "It's not forever or anything, we're just renting it," I say again. "It needs some work, I know that, but it has four bedrooms and a finished basement. It's only a short drive from the ranch, and it's—"

"Perfect," Nova whispers, putting her hand over her heart as if to help herself calm down. She turns to me with the brightest smile, her golden eyes glittering with tears. "You did this for me?"

I wrap her up in my arms. "I'd do anything for you, beautiful."

Nova steps back and reaches out for Isaiah. "Did you know about this too?"

He avoids her gaze and rubs a hand on the back of his neck. "Not at first. Jacob was going to surprise both of us before I ruined everything."

"Hey," Nova says, tugging at his hand and making him look at her.

The fire in her eyes has me all kinds of worked up, but I swallow back my hunger so they can have their moment. Isaiah needs her reassurance more than I need to get my dick wet. Barely.

"I forgave you. I know it'll take time to forgive yourself, but you can start by letting me love you."

Isaiah gathers her up in his arms and rests his forehead on hers. "You always know what to say, princess," he whispers.

"What about me? I seem to remember having a few heart-to-hearts that didn't suck," I complain, lightening the mood.

Nova giggles and Isaiah mumbles some smart-ass remark, making me smirk.

"Anyway, as I was saying. We've got some work to do here, but the guys at the ranch all want to pitch in. Miranda said she'd help us rearrange our furniture to achieve peak feng shui."

"You told my mom?"

"We may have chatted," I shrug. "She was onto something with her green aventurine crystals and my heart or whatever, so I gave her free rein to organize our energy flow."

Nova sighs exasperatedly. "You have no idea what you're getting yourself into."

"As long as I'm getting into you, I don't really give a fuck about anything else," I say, yanking her into my chest and crashing my lips down on hers.

Nova gasps and clutches at my shirt, clinging to me as I kiss the ever-living fuck out of her soft, pretty, pink lips. We've been all sweet kisses and gentle caresses since getting her back, but the time for that is over.

She senses my need, my urgency, and claws up my chest, pushing me against the wall. I growl into her hot little mouth and nip her lips, kissing and sucking and biting my way down her neck. Isaiah steps up behind her and winds his hands in between my body and Nova's, kneading her hips and stomach and helping her roll her curvy body against mine.

"Get on your knees, princess," he whispers harshly into her ear. "Suck Jacob's cock and show him how much you love this house."

Nova whimpers and nods her head, breathing heavily. "Yes, yes, I want it," she stutters out, sinking down in front of me. She looks up at me with those big, beautiful eyes, round and full of lust and love. Nova nibbles on her bottom lip and furrows her brow in concentration as she pops open the button of my jeans. So fucking eager to please.

I brush her silky auburn hair behind her ears so I can see the look on her face when she takes me out. Goddamn, feeling her small hands wrap around my girth has me leaking precum all over my shaft. Nova hums in appreciation and pumps her hand up and down, spreading my arousal with her fingertips.

"Jesus Christ," I grunt, snapping my hips involuntarily.

Nova grins and licks her fucking lips, swirling the tip of her tongue over the head of my cock, massaging the little slit and driving me absolutely insane. I comb my fingers through her hair and hold the sides of her head, guiding her to where I need her most.

She kisses the tip of my dick and giggles when it twitches and dribbles more precum.

"Stop teasing me, kitten," I warn.

"What are you gonna do about it?" she says with a sexy as fuck little grin.

Isaiah wraps his hand around the back of Nova's neck and inches her forward. Nova obeys, opening her mouth and sliding down my dick at a deliciously slow pace. I hiss out a breath and squeeze my eyes shut, letting myself feel her heat, her suction, her little tongue as it massages my cock.

In and out, slowly, slowly, more, more, deeper, fuck, she swallows around me and groans, digging her nails into my ass and holding me there. One second I'm lost in her depths, and the next, she's being ripped away from me.

I snap my eyes open ready to demand her to suck me off, but what I see has me about ready to burst. Isaiah drops his jeans and boxer briefs to the floor and shoves Nova down on all fours so her ass is pointed right at him. He massages her round cheeks and flips her dress up, growling at what he sees.

"No fucking panties, princess?"

I groan and get on my knees as well, positioning my cock in front of Nova's lips while Isaiah settles himself behind her, dipping his fingers inside of that sweet, sticky cunt of hers.

"You both keep—*oh fuck*, yes, right there—you keep ruining them..." Nova trails off on a moan, rocking her hips into Isaiah's hand while lapping at my dick.

"Holy hell, beautiful," I whisper, petting her head and encouraging her to continue.

"You're going to take both of us, aren't you?" Isaiah grunts, lining himself up with her dripping entrance.

"Please," Nova whimpers, widening her legs and opening her mouth so I can take what I need.

I grip her face while Isaiah digs his fingers into her hips. We share a possessive, predatory look, and then we slam our cocks into our whimpering, wanton woman at the same time. Nova screams around my cock, the vibrations echoing throughout my body as I pump into her again and again.

Isaiah slips his hand down Nova's stomach and finds her clit, making our girl tremble and moan. She pops off of my dick and gasps for air, saliva dripping out of her mouth and a feral, hungry look in her eyes. I tangle my fingers in her messy hair and tilt her head up so I can kiss her.

Nova parts her lips and I twist my tongue around hers in a desperate, wild kiss. I feel her body shake with the force of Isaiah's thrusts, and that only turns me on more.

"Fuck, Nova, missed you so damn much, missed everything about you," I murmur into her mouth before kissing her again. When we break apart, Nova slides her hand up and down my throbbing cock and then massages my heavy balls, making my body tense up with the need for release.

"Missed you too, Jacob," she whispers, her breath tickling my overly sensitive skin. "Let me show you how much," she says, right before she takes me into the back of her throat.

Isaiah and I fuck our girl and fill her up in long, powerful strokes. We're working together, the three of us, building each other up and pushing ourselves right to the edge, so close, one more swipe of her tongue, one more hard thrust from Isaiah, one more strangled cry, one more swallow...

"Fuck!" Isaiah roars, jackhammering in and out of Nova as his seed splashes down her thighs. Goddamn, I can smell it, smell the two of them. It has my balls drawing up tight as I ride that sweet, torturous edge.

Nova looks up at me, her mouth stuffed full of my cock, her eyes watering, her needy cries caught in her throat. Beautiful. Ours. Forever.

"Gonna cum now, kitten," I growl. She nods and cracks her jaw open impossibly wider so she can take even more of me.

My orgasm claws up my spine and squeezes all the air from my lungs as I burst down Nova's throat in forceful waves. She gags and swallows, such a good fucking girl, shaking and whimpering as I empty myself inside of her.

Isaiah pulls Nova up so her back is to his front. He grabs her tits over her dress and pinches her nipples, biting down on her neck. I crawl forward and lift the hem of her skirt up, burying my face in between her thighs and sucking on that swollen fucking clit. Hard.

"Yes! Oh shit, oh shit, don't stop, don't..."

I growl and bite down on her little ball of nerves, swallowing down her juices as she cries out and creams all over my tongue. I feel her go limp, but Isaiah holds her up while I keep going, keep sucking on her folds, keep tasting her sweetness. Nova whimpers and tries to twist away from me, but I don't let her. I lick her furiously, sending her crashing into another orgasm, this one more intense than the last, leaving her rattled and panting for air.

I collapse on my back, followed a second later by Nova, who lands on my chest. Isaiah joins us on the floor of our new house, the three of us melting into each other in the best way possible. I comb my fingers through Nova's hair, trying to untangle it a bit, while she traces patterns over my chest. Isaiah rolls to his side and runs a hand up and down Nova's back, kissing the top of her head and snuggling in beside her.

"We're definitely going to have to air this place out before my mom gets here," Nova says so matter-of-factly that I have to laugh.

"Oh yeah? And why is that, kitten?"

She narrows her eyes at me but smiles so brightly I almost forget how to breathe.

"Because it smells like *sex*," she whispers.

Isaiah chuckles deeply, propping himself up on his elbow so he can lean over and kiss Nova's cheek.

"I think your mom probably knows we have sex," he says.

Nova blushes bright red and tries to hide her face in my chest. "I know," she mumbles.

I laugh, hugging her closer and rocking her back and forth. "How are you still so shy about us? It's fucking adorable."

"Just because I don't want to talk to my mom about having crazy monkey sex with my hot twin cowboys doesn't mean I'm *shy*," she protests.

"Fair enough," I concede. "Monkey sex, huh?" I tease.

"Hot twin cowboys?" Isaiah drawls, kissing up her spine.

"Mmhm," Nova purrs, snuggling deeper into me. "Mine. My twin cowboys," she murmurs.

"Yours," Isaiah says.

"All yours, beautiful."

Chapter 17

My mom finished up the last of her treatments and post-op appointments last week, and while she can't be considered in remission for a few more months, the doctors assured us she's well on her way to being completely cancer-free.

I didn't realize all the pent-up emotions and stress I had been carrying about that until we got the good news. I broke down into heaving sobs, right there in the doctor's office. She thought I had heard her wrong at first, but I waved her off. Jacob and Isaiah were there with us, and both of them took such good care of me, of my mom as well.

It's been two weeks since Jacob surprised the hell out of me with the house he rented. I still can't believe it. I'm getting everything I've ever wanted. No, I'm getting way more than I ever could have possibly wanted. I didn't even know I could have two men take care of me, pleasure me, dominate me, and yet love on me so sweetly.

I'm on my way to meet up with Jade and Teagan, finally getting that girls' night we had to reschedule. I smile thinking about how my family has grown so much over the last few weeks. Everyone at Rivera Ranch has welcomed me with open arms, and not only me but my mom as well.

"Nova! Over here!" Jade calls out to me once I walk into Roy's. I smile and go over to their table, giving Jade and Teagan hugs before sitting down.

"How are you feeling? Still having morning sickness?" Teagan asks.

"This week has been better, thank God. How are the kiddos?"

Jade and Teagan take turns updating me on the lives of their kids and how fast they are growing. My cheeks hurt with how much I'm smiling and picturing my kid growing up with friends and a big, happy family. I don't even realize I'm crying until Teagan reaches out and touches my arm.

"What's wrong? I didn't mean to make you cry!"

"I'm just so happy," I sniffle. "And I have all of these hormones making me go crazy."

Jade squeezes my other hand and then starts crying too. "Dammit, look what you've done," she teases. "I've got those crazy hormones too, you know. I can't see someone cry without joining them."

We sip our virgin margaritas and talk about life and love. I'm blown away by the acceptance of everyone at the ranch. There has never been a raised brow or a judgmental look, only smiles and warmth.

"Mind if I steal my girl away?" A deep, sexy voice interrupts our giggles over a funny story Jade was telling. I look up and see Jacob smiling down at me.

"She's all yours." Teagan grins at me, a sparkle of something mischievous in her eyes. Jade looks like she's going to cry again but in a good way. They seem like they know something I don't, but I trust that it's a good surprise. Usually, I'm not a fan of surprises and the unknown, but I feel safe and confident with these people. My family.

A few minutes later, we're pulling up to our house. Moving in has been a slow process, but we're almost all the way done. We spend about half our nights here, a few nights at the old cabin, and a few nights at the cottage with my mom.

"You've been awfully quiet, should I be nervous?" I half tease.

Jacob grins at me, kissing my knuckles before helping me out of the truck.

The sun is just beginning to set, the orange and pink hues silhouetting our house against the brilliant light and rolling fields. I notice the sidewalk and stairs leading up to the front door are lined with dimly lit lanterns and flower petals.

"What is all of this?" I whisper, slowly moving forward and taking it all in.

"Go inside and find out," Jacob murmurs from behind me, placing his hand on the small of my back to guide me the rest of the way inside.

When I open the door, my jaw drops. Almost every surface is covered in candles and bouquets of wildflowers. There's a fire going in the fireplace and I notice a new couch and a plush, fuzzy rug that looks comfortable enough to sleep on.

Isaiah steps into the living room and gets down on one knee. My hands go to my mouth to cover up my gasp. This isn't happening, is it? Jacob kisses my temple and steps around me so he can get down on one knee, too. He reaches out for my right hand while Isaiah takes my left.

"Nova, you haven't been in our lives for very long, but we already know we can't live without you," Jacob says, his eyes a bit misty as he takes a deep breath. "I love your gorgeous smile, the way it lights up your eyes and takes over your whole face. I love that you put me in my place and don't fall for any of my shit. I love how kind and giving you are, how sweet and sassy, how truly beautiful you are inside and out. Will you marry me?"

Before I can answer, Isaiah squeezes my hand and places it on his cheek. It's such a sweet, submissive gesture from this giant, brooding man who has captured my heart.

"I love you in a way that scares me. It's so big, so all-consuming, it's hard to breathe sometimes. I almost ruined the best thing that ever happened to me, but I'll spend the rest of my days filling your life with so much light and love, you won't have a chance to remember any of the pain I caused. We might not be able to have an official marriage certificate, but we are yours, forever, in every sense of the word. Nova, my princess, my fucking queen, will you marry me?"

He pulls out a gorgeous princess cut diamond ring and places it on my ring finger before kissing it and looking up at me with such love and anticipation.

"I..." My voice cracks with emotion and I fall to my knees, throwing my arms around my two men and letting them catch me. "Yes, yes, I want whatever you'll give me. I love you both so much."

"Everything, we'll give you everything, kitten," Jacob whispers, his lips inches from mine. I close the distance between us, my lips melting into his while Isaiah sweeps my hair to the side and kisses my neck.

Our gentle touches and sweet declarations of love turn heated and desperate. Four hands roam over my body, squeezing my flesh, twisting my hair, and wrapping around my throat.

I moan and lift my arms up, letting Isaiah take my shirt off. We stand up, stripping out of our clothes, stealing kisses and lingering touches. Everywhere they touch me sparks with a delicious ache, a longing for more, a need so deep inside me I know it will take both of them to satisfy my hunger.

We make our way over to the new couch, a sly grin playing at my lips.

"What are you thinking about, kitten?" Jacob asks, trailing his fingers down my body until he's cupping my pussy in a possessive grip. I moan and squirm at his touch, my walls clamping around his thick fingers.

"The best way to break in the new couch. And the rug. And every room in this house."

Isaiah groans from behind me, nipping at my shoulder and licking away the sting. "I have a few ideas," he practically purrs, sliding his hand down my spine, tickling every nerve ending before he slips two fingers into my slit, circling my tight little asshole.

"Yes, more..." I breathe out, bucking my hips as I seek more friction, more of whatever is going to happen next.

Isaiah sits down on the couch behind me, skimming his nose down my spine and nipping at the globes of my ass while his fingers grip my hips possessively. Jacob cups my chin, drawing my face towards his so he can kiss me.

Isaiah replaces Jacob's fingers in my pussy, rubbing them up and down my soaking slit, gathering up my juices and circling my clit. I gasp and fall forward slightly, resting my forehead on Jacob's shoulder while Isaiah sinks two fingers inside of my pulsing cunt. He groans and removes his fingers, pulling them back towards my ass.

"I'm gonna take you right here, princess," Isaiah's deep voice rumbles as he pushes his fingers inside my back entrance.

At the same time, Jacob grabs my hair and tilts my head up, searing his lips onto mine, branding me with his flavor. His tongue slides in and out of my mouth in the same steady rhythm of Isaiah's fingers.

Jacob breaks away from my mouth and blazes a trail of kisses down my neck and over my collarbone until he's sucking on my nipples, back and forth, pinching the pebbled peaks between his teeth and then licking away the sting.

I buck my hips, forcing more of Isaiah's thick fingers inside of my ass. He grunts and shoves a third finger deep inside, twisting them together until it burns, until my nerves singe with heat, until my skin is coated in fire and my core erupts into flames. My climax claims me, body and soul.

Jacob holds me steady, grunting into the side of my neck, his muscles flexing as I tremble and cry out against him. "You like that, kitten?" he rasps, licking and biting the tender skin on my neck. "Like coming around his fingers in your ass? You're gonna love when he has his cock up in your tight little hole. Want to feel it?"

"Yes," I whimper, trying to nod my head but not having enough concentration to do anything but surrender.

Isaiah massages my hips in his large hands and then cups my cheeks, spreading me wide open for him. I feel his breath on my most private place, then his tongue as it circles around my tight ring of muscles. He guides me to sit down on his lap, but he stills my movement when I'm perched right above his cock.

"I'm gonna break your tight little ass in, princess. It's ours now, all of you belongs to us, every fucking inch, every drop of pleasure, every tear, every hope, every smile, it's ours."

"Yours, I'm yours, I want it," I whisper, tears stinging my eyes, though not from fear or anxiety. I'm overwhelmed by how much they love me, and from the depths of their souls. I feel so cherished, so used, but only in the best way possible.

I cling to Jacob while Isaiah positions my legs on the outside of his and then slowly guides my ass down on his massive cock. There's so much pressure, so much tension, so much need vibrating between our bodies I swear I'm about to pass out.

"Breathe, just breathe for me, sweet girl," Isaiah murmurs into the back of my neck. I do as he says and take in air, willing my muscles to relax.

"That's it, beautiful," Jacob encourages, removing my hands from his hips and guiding them up over my head until I'm gripping Isaiah's har. "Let him have control. Make him feel good while I make you feel good, okay, kitten?"

I nod my head, but I can't really process his words. Isaiah grabs my thighs and snaps his hips, filling me up and tearing me open while I scream and rip at his hair. Fuck, it hurts, but I'm somehow close to coming already. Isaiah grunts and holds me in place while he grinds that thick dick deep, so deep inside of me.

"I've got you, Nova, you're doing so good, so good, sweet girl, fuck me, you feel amazing," he whispers, half pained, half in awe. I'm feeling the exact same way.

I feel Isaiah spread me open even more as he widens his legs in between mine. Then Jacob's warm breath skates across my chest, his tongue darting out to lick my aching nipples before trailing down my body. I'm aware of every single nerve ending his mouth touches, down, down, down, tongue, teeth, lips, again, lower, again...

Then Jacob sucks my clit into his mouth and shoves two fingers in my pussy and I cum harder than I ever have.

Isaiah roars and fucks up into me, sawing his huge cock in and out of my ass as Jacob eats out my pussy with a ferocious need. One of my hands twists in Isaiah's hair while the other reaches out and grips Jacob.

I'm completely consumed by them, taken so thoroughly, surrendering my body and heart to every thrust, every lick, every rough touch, and tender kiss. I'm about to cum again when Jacob stands up suddenly and takes me with him.

I'm spun around and then I'm straddling Jacob's lap as he lies down on the plush rug in front of the fireplace. He sheaths himself inside of me in one hard thrust, entering me completely and stretching my pussy wide open.

I cry out in shock as overwhelming pleasure rushes through me. Rocking my hips back and forth, I grind against Jacob's monster cock, loving the way he shudders underneath me.

"I couldn't wait," he grits out, cupping my breasts and pushing them together so he can lick and nip at my cleavage as he tears my pussy up.

I feel Isaiah's heat behind me, and then one large hand rests between my shoulder blades as he pushes me forward so I have to brace myself on my forearms on either side of Jacob's head.

"Fuck yes," Isaiah groans, massaging my ass and helping me grind down on Jacob. "Gonna fill you up all the way, princess. Can you handle two cocks, my dirty girl? Two big cocks just for you, worshiping you every goddamn day?"

"P-please," I whimper, bowing my back and bucking my hips to show him how much I want him, too.

Jacob cups the back of my neck, demanding a kiss from me. He pries a moan out of my lips as he kisses and fucks me like we're on fire. Isaiah grips my hips and eases inside of me. Jacob pulls out and then pushes back in when Isaiah leaves me. They take turns thrusting into me, hitting places I didn't know I had, bringing me higher and higher, so high I'm afraid I'm going to shatter when I finally come down.

Jacob grunts and slams into me over and over, his movements becoming jerky and uneven. I rest my sweaty forehead on his, needing this connection too while my body is being used and ripped apart savagely.

"I've got you, Nova, my beautiful girl. You feel fucking amazing. I love you so much, need you so much, love."

I whimper and nod my head against his, squeezing my eyes shut and falling into the rhythm of my men filling me and fucking me like we were made for each other.

We grunt and groan together, working as one to reach ultimate bliss. Isaiah pistons in and out of me while Jacob grinds his massive length deep inside of my pussy, rubbing my clit with the base of his cock and making me spasm and clench around him.

The air is thick with the smell of sex and the obscene, sloppy wet smacking sounds of our bodies coming together over and over, joining as one. My orgasm bubbles up from the very depths of my being, pooling in my belly and trickling out into every cell. My lungs fill with air and I hold my breath as it takes me under, plunging me into darkness, bliss rocking me back and forth in violent waves.

Jacob shouts out a curse and explodes inside of me, triggering another climax to match his own. Seconds later, Isaiah snarls and cracks his hips against my ass before emptying himself of every last drop. We cum together, our combined orgasms spilling out of me and coating all of us until we're a mess of sweat, cum, tangled limbs, and ragged breaths.

"Holy shit," Jacob whispers once he's caught his breath. He turns his head to look at me, his eyes filled with awe and complete satisfaction. "I mean, just... Holy shit," he says again.

Isaiah lets out a muffled groan of agreement from where he's lying face down on the rug.

I laugh softly, trying to lift my head up. No such luck. I'm too exhausted to move an inch. Jacob scoops me up and lays me across his chest, kissing the top of my head and stroking my back.

"You okay, beautiful?"

"Mmhm," I mumble, snuggling closer to him.

Isaiah shuffles slightly and turns so he's facing me. His deep green eyes skim over my prone body and then he reaches out to trace my curves.

"I think you broke me," he teases.

I somehow find the strength to grab his hand and kiss his fingers. "How can I fix it?" I whisper while sucking his middle finger into my mouth.

"Princess..." Isaiah groans, half in pain, half aroused.

"Holy hell, kitten, are you ready to go again?" Jacob asks, still in a daze himself.

I rest my head back down on his chest and lace my fingers with Isaiah's keeping him close. "Boys, I don't think I'm going to be able to move from this spot for at least twelve hours."

They both laugh and give me sweet kisses. "That's okay, beautiful. We have forever."

"Forever," Isaiah agrees, running his thumb over my engagement ring.

"Forever," I echo, letting the word sink inside of me and settle into my very core. "I like the sound of that."

Epilogue

Isaiah

"I'm sure glad we decided to renovate this barn and use it as an event space," Jade muses before taking a sip of her sparkling cider.

"We've gotten some good use out of it so far," Noah replies. "Though if we keep giving our staff free rein to throw weddings here, we'll be losing money before we know it."

Jade slaps him playfully in the chest, and he grabs her hand up and kisses her palm. "We're doing alright as it is. In fact, I just posted the new positions we're hiring for, and there's already a flood of applications for event staff, a second chef, and a few ranch hands."

"Ranch hands? You trying to replace us?" I ask.

"Not at all. But I figure you three will need some time alone, and when the baby comes, your whole life will change," Jade says dreamily. Noah kisses his wife and rubs her baby belly, though she's barely showing. I long to do the same to my wife.

I scan the decked-out barn for my bride and see her twirling around the dance floor with Jacob. Nova throws her head back and laughs as Jacob spins her around and then dips her low. God, I can't believe I get to spend the rest of my life with them.

Jacob is good for her in a way I never could be. He can get her to laugh and smile and relax no matter the circumstance. Though, these days Nova is all smiles all the time. I like to think I contributed to that, too. I provide a calm and peaceful space for Nova to relax in and be herself. We balance each other out in a way other people might not understand, but that's okay.

After Nova officially moved in with us, Jade asked if she would consider being the office manager of Rivera Ranch. She was over the moon about the job offer and agreed immediately. When Nova told us about it, she dissolved into a pile of tears, which tore me apart.

Apparently, there are happy tears, which Nova explained to us after she calmed down a bit.

Nova wanted to get married the day after we proposed, but Jade and Teagan convinced her to hold off for a few weeks so they could do up the barn and throw us a real party. Between the three of them, they got this place looking like a fairy tale dream wedding with soft, sparkling lights, lace, tons of fresh flowers, and a massive cake that Teagan spent several days constructing.

I wouldn't care if we got married in a ditch on the side of the road or in Buckingham Palace, as long as it's Nova and Jacob at my side. That being said, everything has been perfect. We didn't have the traditional ceremony, but we did exchange rings and vows under the big weeping willow next to the stream on the north side of the ranch. Noah got up and said a few words and then directed everyone to the feast set up in the barn.

I never knew my heart could be so full, but standing up there with Jacob and committing our lives to Nova in front of our friends and family is something I will treasure for the rest of my days.

Swallowing around the sudden lump in my throat, I make my way over to Nova and Jacob. Never before have I been overcome with such emotion, such love, such longing. Jacob grins at me and Nova gives me a heart-stopping smile, her golden eyes glittering with joy.

Jacob spins Nova out of his arms, straight into mine. I catch her and kiss her right there on the dance floor. When we break apart, Nova cups my face in her hands and wipes away a single tear that somehow escaped from the corner of my eye. Well, damn. There really are happy tears.

"I love you so much, Isaiah."

"I love you too, my sweet girl. So fucking much."

"What about me? Any love for ol' Jacob?"

Nova giggles and I grunt.

"Love you too, Jacob, I—"

She stops short when the music changes, and then she bursts out laughing. "Is this *Beautiful* by Snoop Dogg?!" she laughs, looking between Jacob and me.

Jacob shrugs. "It felt fitting," he grins.

Nova grabs our hands and leads us to the middle of the dance floor, where she throws her hands up and urges us to dance with her. We gladly do.

I can't say I ever thought I'd be dancing in a barn to Snoop Dogg with my wife - whom I share with my twin brother - but then again, nothing about Nova has been expected. I wouldn't have it any other way.

Looking around the dance floor, I see Noah dancing with Jade, holding her close and whispering something that makes her blush. I avert my gaze, smirking to myself, and catch sight of Teagan and Knox swaying back and forth. There's so much love in this room, it's humbling.

I've never been the spiritual type, despite Miranda's best efforts, but in this moment, I feel connected to every single person here. I know we will face difficult times together, that life will throw us curve balls and even cut us off at the knees at times, but knowing I have Nova and Jacob, as well as the support of our friends... Well, it makes me feel damn near invincible.

Nova turns her head and looks at me over her shoulder, her eyes lit up with a warm smile. I swear this woman can read my mind and knows exactly what I'm thinking.

"Thank you both for making me so happy," she murmurs, kissing me and then Jacob.

"We will every damn day, beautiful," Jacob says.

"Always, princess. Always."

Also by Cameron Hart

Check out my other popular series and books!
Mafia, MC, & Bodyguard Romance:
<u>Moscatelli Crime Family Series</u>[1]
<u>Di Salvo Crime Family Series</u>[2]
<u>Chaos MC series</u>[3]
<u>Savage Ride</u>[4]
Mountain Man Romance:
<u>Men of Blackthorne Mountain Series</u>[5]
<u>Bear's Tooth Mountain Men Series</u>[6]
Cowboy & Small Town Romance:
<u>Roped in by Love Series</u>[7]

---

1. https://books2read.com/u/mqBaze

2. https://books2read.com/u/m0odzW

3. https://books2read.com/u/bMVAOk

4. https://books2read.com/u/bMVlG7

5. https://books2read.com/u/3RYDvB

6. https://books2read.com/u/mVel7A

7. https://books2read.com/u/3RYlBY